Praise for Alannah Lynne and her novels

Savin' Me

"Let me just say that giving a five wine glass toast is not something I do often. So, not only am I thrilled to give this book the proverbial five star because it was an extremely well written book that pulled at the heart strings, but also because it's an indie author with a self pubbed book! Thank you Alannah Lynne for such a great story!"

–Reading Between The Wines Book Club

"*Savin' Me* is the perfect example of a well written romance novel. The characters are complex, the plot line realistic, the sex scenes gratifying, and the happily ever after we all enjoy."

–Guilty Pleasure Book Reviews

"So I sit here at my laptop and all I can say is WOW!! This book was absolutely amazing."

–Twinsie Talk Book Reviews

"Alannah Lynne's book exudes sex and desire. From the very first few pages, readers will be overheated and longing for more."

–AriesGrlReview.com

"Ms. Lynne's characters are able to explore real feelings and desires and allow the story to unfold at a pace that kept me interested and cheering for their HEA."

–TheJeepDiva.com

Last Call

"Ms. Lynne brings depth to her characters and stories. As I read the book, I could picture in my head the places and people that she described. Her style of writing is edgy that can be transcribed into any small beach front to the largest of cities. I look forward to reading another book and series. A must read."

–TheJeepDiva.com

"Both the suspense and romance are well written and keep the reader engaged and tense waiting to see what happens next."

–MyBookAddictionReviews.com

"I love this author's voice; her characters feel like friends, her setting feels like a place I could call home, and no doubt her wicked sex scenes make you feel all kinds of things!"

–Guilty Pleasures Book Reviews

"I love the details in this book. I was so into the story by the details, I felt like I was THERE watching/feeling the events happen."

–Twinsie Talk Book Reviews

"This book provides romance and suspense and it all takes place in a small, quiet beach community. Oh and the intricate details of the bar, the personality of the people and the random smells from Georgetown, South Carolina are accurate and paint a 'real' picture for those who have not lived in a small town beach community."

–AriesGrlBookReview.com

Savin' Me

Book #1 in the Heat Wave Series

Alannah Lynne

Kim –
Thank you for your
friendship and all of your
support! Peace and love,
Alannah

Dedication

Dedicated to my parents.
Thank you for your unwavering belief
and faith in me. I love you!

Acknowledgements

A friend recently said, "It takes a village to get me published." Whew… ain't it the truth! There are so many people that touch my life on a daily basis and all have played a part, in one way or another, in getting me to this point. I couldn't possibly list everyone, but there are a few I absolutely must acknowledge.

First, the Plotmonkeys (Carly Phillips, Janelle Denison, Julie Leto, Leslie Kelly) for introducing me to the fabulous, amazing world of romance!! You'll never know the influence you've had over the years, or how much I appreciate the kindness you've shown me!!

Thank you, Amy Eye and Cassie McCown at The Eyes for Editing, for making the words pretty, and especially for fixing my horrible punctuation!! And what would pretty words be without an amazing cover? Thanks Tricia "Pickyme" Schmitt for your usual awesomeness!

Thanks to Leagh Christensen for making order from the chaos. And where would I be without my board of directors, also affectionately known as my Mistresses: Amanda McFarland, Cheri Biddix, Liz Henderson, and Michelle Unger. Thank you, from the bottom of my heart, for being my BOD, beta readers, and most especially, my friends!

When I put on my writer hat, I tend to get lost in my fictional worlds and sometimes forget the real one. I need to thank my amazing husband and sons for forgiving all of those burned (or forgotten) meals, and for keeping me in clean clothes. I love you guys!! Thanks for sharing this journey with me.

But most of all, thank YOU, the reader!! Without you, there wouldn't be a need for me.

Chapter One

---

*O*h man, not the strawberry... not the strawberry... Aw, shit.
Erik Monteague clenched his jaw and steeled his defenses
against the impending carnal assault. The laughing guests, jazz
band, overflowing food tables—everything at the Sinclair Marketing Group
open house faded into the woodwork as his field of vision narrowed down
to ruby lips and the damn lucky strawberry about to be sucked into them.

Her pink tongue flicked across full, luscious lips, then scooped a bead
of chocolate from the bottom of the large, ripe fruit. She opened her
mouth, slid the berry inside, and wrapped her lips around it.

Good God Almighty. Erik shifted his stance and stifled a moan. "I can't
believe I'm jealous of a piece of fruit."

A familiar chuckle pierced his lust-filled haze, causing his pinpoint
vision to snap back to wide-angle view. From the corner of his eye, he
spotted his best friend, Steve Vex, making like a bartender, serving up a
beer.

"What's up?" Steve asked, laughing.

The smirk on Steve's face proved the question was rhetorical, so rather
than answering the jackass, Erik swiped one of the beers. "Perfect timing."

"Yeah, you looked like you might be overheating." Steve tipped his
bottle in *her* direction and hitched his chin. "I've never seen her before.
Who is she?"

Who is she?

Erik stared at Steve for a moment, perplexed by the simple question. It
shouldn't have required much thought, but Erik, always a straight-shooting,
tell-it-like-it-is kind of guy, found himself hedging.

He pinched the bridge of his nose and squeezed his eyes shut, trying to
ward off the explosive memories of her and their night together.

Her mouth—warm and slick—wrapped tightly around him...

*Her beneath him, bottom lip caught between her teeth in an effort to hold back her
screams... Her mouth dropping open to gasp for air as she cried out her release...*

Him waking and reaching for her, only to find himself alone...

He swallowed hard and scrubbed a hand down his face. "I don't know who she is," he said, somewhat truthfully. After all, just because you knew someone intimately didn't mean you *knew* them.

Steve quirked a pierced eyebrow. "Yeah, I think I'm going to have to call bullshit on that."

At times, having a friend who was closer than a brother was a true blessing. This wasn't one of those times. "Sometimes you're a real pain in the ass."

Steve's lopsided grin grew to obnoxious proportions. "Yep," he said, "it's something I live for, especially where you're concerned." He took a sip of beer and waited. And waited. And when Erik didn't elaborate, he pressed the issue further. "Seriously. What's the deal?"

Erik took a long drink of beer, then studied the floor and fought the urge to shuffle his feet like a teenager being grilled by a suspicious parent. He and Steve had been friends since the first day of kindergarten, when they'd both gotten into trouble for standing underneath the monkey bars, sneaking peeks up the girls' dresses. In their twenty-seven-year friendship Erik had never kept anything from Steve.

Until now.

Unwilling to analyze why he wanted to keep her identity, or the scope of their relationship, private, when he'd never worried about that kind of thing before, he grinned slyly and said, "My friend, we have shared many things. But whatever I might know about her, I'm keeping to myself."

"Damn." All traces of amusement dropped from Steve's face, and he whistled low. "That sounds serious."

Erik bristled at what he suspected could maybe, possibly be a spec of truth, if he allowed it to go that far. But he recovered quickly and turned it into a joke. Nailing on a smile, he said, "It is." He took a moment to enjoy surfing the shock waves rolling off his friend before adding, "Serious lust. You know, the kind that results in sex that's mind-altering, not life-altering."

Shit. The instant the words left his mouth, he knew he'd taken the sarcasm too far. He'd left an opening big enough to drive a truck through, and, as expected, Steve barreled in. "Dammit, Erik, it's been ten years. When are you gonna let it go and move on?"

Erik rolled his head in a circle, attempting to loosen the muscles in his neck and shoulders that'd suddenly snapped into tight bands. They'd had this conversation too many times to count, and he didn't want to have it again.

Not tonight.

Not ever.

Rather than delve into the past—a past he couldn't change or forget—he directed his attention across the room to something much more pleasant.

Kat.

He chuckled as he considered for the first time the possibility she might have given him a false name. That would certainly explain why, on all of his subsequent trips to Charlotte and multiple attempts to find her, he'd come up empty.

The name fit her so well, he found himself hoping she hadn't lied. Tall and lithe, her movements were fluid and graceful, like those of a cat. And when stroked just right, she damn near purred. He scowled. She'd also crawled under his skin and become a constant source of irritation—like cat scratch fever.

He crossed his arms over his chest and leaned against the wall, studying her. She looked different than she had the night they'd met, and at first glance, he thought his mind was playing tricks on him. But the more he watched her move through the crowd, mixing and mingling and interacting, the more obvious it became. Her conservative business suit couldn't hide her tempting curves or disguise the way her body moved with a natural sensuality.

She still screamed "sex," and he still wanted her to the point of aching.

His stomach—and khakis—tightened as more unwelcome memories of her unbridled passion assaulted him. Her green eyes, locked within his gaze; her black hair falling across his chest while she rode him to oblivion. He'd almost forgotten all the reasons he avoided relationships and nearly professed true love that night.

It was probably for the best that she'd snuck out on him while he slept. It had prevented him from doing something foolish. Like falling for her.

"Hey, Romeo."

Startled from his thoughts, Erik jumped. The wicked gleam in Steve's eyes set Erik's nerves on edge, and his irritation flared. "What?"

"I hate to wake you from your wet dream, but Elise has been watching you watch… whoever she is. And now Elise is headed this way." He laughed and slapped Erik on the back. "You're on your own with this one, brother, I'm out."

Shit.

Erik closed his eyes and gulped his beer, wishing he had a keg tapped straight into his veins. There wasn't enough alcohol in the world to make Elise Winstead tolerable, and the only reason he tried to be civil was out of respect for their mothers' friendship.

Elise stopped in front of him, crossed her arms under her large, surgically enhanced breasts, and pierced him with an icy look recognized by males from every corner of the globe.

Rather than play games or dally around, he decided to get straight to the point and be done with her. "What do you want, Elise?"

"Nothing, really." She pecked a talon against her cheek. "It's just that… Well, I couldn't help but notice your interest in my competition."

Despite his desire to stay aloof, Erik felt his eyebrows rise in surprise. How could Elise and Kat be in competition for anything? One was like a Rolls Royce: compact with overdone curves, high maintenance, and pretentious as hell. The other—he flicked a glance to Kat—was like his Harley: sleek, commanded attention, represented wild abandon, and provided the ride of a life.

"Competition?" he asked, hesitant to encourage further conversation, but curious enough about Kat's presence at SMG to risk it.

"The new account executive Rusty hired." She looked at Kat with a truckload of disgust. "She's from a big agency in Charlotte, and she's got ninety days to prove she's better than me." She snorted. "As if." Mumbling more to herself than speaking directly to him, she said, "I just don't understand why she'd leave a large agency to come here. Something's fishy."

Erik suspected he knew why Kat left her old job, probably for the same reason she'd been in that bar drinking the night they'd met. But no way in hell would he arm Elise with that kind of ammunition against Kat, or anyone else for that matter. If she was going to be a seething boil on someone's ass, she'd have to do it without his help.

"What's her name?" he asked, pleased to hear he'd managed to sound casual and only moderately interested.

"Kat Owens." Elise shuddered. "Appropriate really—I hate cats. They're sneaky and nasty."

As if sensing she were the topic of conversation, Kat began scanning the crowd while continuing to pick at the food on her plate. Her gaze skimmed past Elise and settled on Erik as she took a bite from another strawberry.

Her eyes widened and she froze in place, strawberry stem caught between her finger and thumb, half of a berry sticking out of her mouth. It would have been humorous if his nerves hadn't been skittering along a razor's edge of irritation.

And if she hadn't started choking.

He'd already taken three steps in her direction when she grabbed her water goblet and managed a few sips. The coughing subsided and she appeared okay, so he forced the tension from his body and resumed his relaxed stance against the wall.

When she glanced at him again, probably hoping he'd been an apparition or a figment of her imagination, he tried to smile. But the question that had plagued him for so long—*Why'd you run out on me like that?*—turned his smile feral.

Her shoulders sagged as she dropped her gaze to the floor, then slipped her feet into her previously discarded shoes.

Elise tilted her head to the side and stared at Kat as she hustled to a small group standing nearby. *Shit.* He could see the wheels in Elise's conniving mind turning and smell the rubber burning.

"Well, that was… interesting." She turned back and studied him, steady and unblinking. "Do you know her?"

With Steve, he'd felt guilty for fudging the truth and had needed to justify his evasion. With Elise, he had no problem flat-out lying. "Nope. Should I?"

Elise narrowed her eyes and studied him. "I don't know."

He knew she wanted to say more. To ask more. But she wasn't known as Queen of Scheme for nothing, and after years of practice, she knew how to hold her cards close to her disproportionately large chest.

Her nose practically twitched as she sniffed the air for clues, knowing there had to be more to this story than she'd been told. She didn't even try to be nonchalant about her devious intentions as she said, "Well, it's been fun… and intriguing, but I've got to go. Things to do and all." She gave a little finger wave and said, "Ta-ta," then headed off in search of a pot to stir.

Erik rubbed a hand over his eyes and drew in a deep, erratic breath. Part of him, the part that had spent the past thirteen months looking for Kat, wanted to yell *Hell yeah!* at his good fortune of finding her again. Looking just as beautiful and sexy as she'd been the night they met, no less.

But dammit, he'd wanted to find her in Charlotte. With him living at the coast, that put the entire state of North Carolina and a five-hour drive between them, thereby limiting the feasibility of establishing what could be misconstrued as a real relationship.

Especially since he didn't do relationships—at least not any that lasted for more than twelve hours. And while he enjoyed more than his fair share of female companions, he always made sure there were no misunderstandings about what to expect after those twelve hours ended. That wasn't to say he wouldn't sleep with a woman more than once. But he always put enough time between encounters to make sure everyone knew where things stood.

And he never spent time thinking about them between visits.

Until Kat.

He hadn't been able to forget her or let go of hoping to see her again. Now, here she was in his hometown. Looking very much like she belonged and very much like she intended to stay. And that presented a problem. The fire between them burned too hot, and he doubted he'd be able to ignore it any more now than he'd been able to ignore it thirteen months ago.

So where did that leave him?

Avoid her and hope the simmering embers eventually cooled and she became a distant memory? Or work her out of his system by picking up where they'd left off?

Naked.

For all that he didn't know, one thing he knew for sure. Before he made any decisions about the future, he needed an answer to the question that had driven him nearly insane for the past thirteen months. Why had she walked out on him without so much as a good-bye kiss or a *kiss my ass?*

***

Kat Owens surveyed the surrounding scene. So this was it. Her new life. A new town, new job, new friends, new everything. All for the opportunity of becoming Vice President of Client Services for Sinclair Marketing Group.

Standing within striking range of the corporate ladder's top rung didn't feel quite like she thought it would. Somehow she pictured herself light as a feather and floating on air. Not weighed down and miserable.

Maybe it was the stuffy clothes and uncomfortable shoes. Maybe it was the pantyhose cutting her lu-lu in half—it was difficult to feel light and airy when important body parts were at risk of permanent damage.

It might be those things, but deep in her heart, she suspected it was more than those superficial discomforts.

She looked around at the various mix of agency staff, clients, and vendors—all here for the supposed purpose of celebrating SMG's move into their new offices. It looked nice, neat, and polite on the surface. Regular people playing nicely, shaking hands, telling jokes, and laughing. Sharing a few—but not too many—personal stories.

But if one looked at these interactions with a microscope, they'd see the ugly truth of advertising life. She supposed all businesses were competitive and cutthroat, but few reached the pinnacle of advertising. In advertising, your best friend would set you up, cut you down, and steal your job. That was tough to beat.

Handshakes and nice-to-meet-yas took place in most polite circles, but not much about this job included any real sincerity or concern for the people you met. It was all about getting what you wanted, and to hell with everyone else.

The hardest part of her job would be the suck-up ass-kissing required to get and keep an account—that's where the laughing and joke telling came in. And the personal stories… those were told to prove you were actually a human being. Sometimes in this business it was difficult to know for sure.

But right now, she was tired and wanted nothing more than to go home, shed the office armor, and crawl into bed. However, as the future VP of Client Services, it was critical she familiarize herself with all of the agency's clients. This event coincided perfectly with her move to Riverside and gave her the opportunity to meet most of the clients all at once. So, until the last guest had their fill of food and drink and headed out the door, she was stuck.

Rusty Sinclair, owner and president of SMG, had spared no expense in throwing this open house celebration to show off his pride and joy—the restored Victorian that now housed the SMG offices. And nowhere was it more evident than in the overflowing food tables.

Shrimp, every color vegetable known to man, stuffed mushrooms, meatballs, and fruit galore sat awaiting a taker. But what appealed to her most were the chocolate-covered strawberries. Actually, it was the chocolate that had her mouth watering, but she could hardly run her finger along the inside of the bowl, or hang her head under the flowing chocolate fountain, so she was forced to take the strawberries, too.

Since leaving this shindig wasn't an option, her best bet was to find a secluded corner where she could drop the smile, slip off her shoes to give her poor, aching feet a break, and take a few deep breaths.

And soothe her soul with chocolate.

She picked a few of the larger berries—because they held more chocolate—loaded them down, then stacked them on her small plate. Settling into an empty corner of the lobby, she kicked off her shoes and sagged in relief against the wall. She picked up a berry, licked her lips, then slid the fruit into her watering mouth, savoring the mixture of sweet, smooth chocolate and tart strawberry.

Oh God, that's good.

After several moments of delectable bliss, the hair on the back of her neck began to prickle. For the past thirty minutes, she'd had the strangest sensation of being watched, and the feeling became too strong to ignore.

She grabbed another berry and casually scanned the crowd. She'd just bitten down, once again enjoying the near-orgasmic feeling of the thick chocolate rolling across her tongue, when she stumbled across a brilliant-blue gaze boring straight into her.

Ohmigod!

Her heart stuttered, her stomach plummeted, and she gasped at the sight of him. Chocolate and strawberry juice shot to the back of her throat, and she began to choke. She yanked the mangled strawberry from her mouth, stifled the coughing as best as she could, then grabbed her glass of water. After a few sips, she had the coughing under control, but her heart rate and breathing remained out of step.

She'd give just about anything to convince herself it wasn't him, but she'd never mistake or forget those eyes. She saw them every night in her dreams and often in daydreams. Even on a cellular level, she recognized them, and everything feminine within her came alive.

Maybe he doesn't recognize me.

Just because she'd spent the last thirteen months reliving every second of their incredible night together didn't mean he had. However, as she flicked her gaze back to him, that tiny fragment of hope slipped away and was replaced with dismay.

The million-watt smile that had played so easily on his mouth the night they'd met was gone, and a severe scowl took its place. Oh yeah, he recognized her and he wasn't happy. In fact, he looked downright pissed.

She didn't know which was worse: him not recognizing her, or him recognizing her, but being so obviously unhappy to see her. A heavy sadness settled over her as she dropped her gaze to the floor, righted her shoes, and slipped her feet into them.

What's a girl gotta do to catch a freakin' break?

The last two weeks had been hell. Between quitting her job—the only job she'd known since college—packing her apartment in a heated rush, and moving from the big city of Charlotte to the small, coastal town of Riverside, where she didn't know anyone besides her new boss, she was operating on a tightly stretched rope.

And at this moment, she heard the faint tearing as a few more strands unraveled and gave way beneath her.

She spotted Maggie and Seth, two of her coworkers, talking with a sales rep from a local radio station that she'd met earlier in the evening. Needing to know Erik's connection to the agency, she casually made her way to them. If luck was on her side, she'd find that no one knew him. He'd be a lost soul who had wandered into the wrong party and decided to stay for a beer.

She slipped into a space between Seth, the very talented and very gay art director, and Maggie, the equally talented and very northern copywriter. She patiently waited for a break in the conversation and when the opportunity presented itself, said, "I think I've been introduced to almost everyone, but there's one gentleman I haven't met yet. I wondered if anyone could tell me who he is."

"I'm sure between all of us," Maggie said, waving her hand around the circle, "we know everyone here. Riverside's not that big a place."

In addition to being talented and northern, Maggie was also, apparently, the queen of understatements. Kat's previous apartment complex had been bigger than the entire town of Riverside.

"I don't want to turn around and be obvious, but he was standing with Elise a minute ago. Around six feet tall, dark hair that's kind of curly and unruly—"

"Rock-star stubble covering a strong jawline and gorgeous blue eyes?"

Kat bit her bottom lip and cut her eyes to Seth. He didn't hide his sexual orientation, but never had his excessive gayness been more evident.

"Damn, Seth," Maggie said. "Even men think Erik's hot?"

Seth looked offended. "Of course. Every gay man in town has the goal of being the one who turns him."

Kat burst out laughing, then threw her hand over her mouth. Erik was as hetero as they came, and there wasn't a chance in hell of turning him. Thank God.

Sexual genius like his couldn't possibly play both sides of the fence, and what a shame it would be for womankind if he did. He had long fingers and strong, capable hands. She'd expected the jagged scars on his palms—the ones he'd flat-out refused to discuss—to be rough, like calluses. But his touch was soft, and he knew exactly where, when, and how to stroke a woman's body to elicit sensations and feelings never before discovered.

At least that's what he'd done to her. And just thinking about it caused dampness in her palms and… other places that had no business getting damp at the moment.

She needed to get a grip. Now wasn't the time to remember, and it sure as hell wasn't the place for a reaction. She now knew Erik was an equal-opportunity sex magnet, but she still didn't know his relationship to the agency. "Who is he? Is he a client?"

"His name is Erik Monteague," Maggie said. "His family owns Monteague Boats, and he's one of our larger clients."

Damn, damn, damn.

"Mmm… hmmm… I imagine he is." Seth had taken on a stereotypical gay man pose—hip cocked to the side, one arm crossed over his stomach while his free hand held a glass of wine to his lips. His eyes were hooded and appreciative as he stared at Erik.

"Life offers few guarantees, Seth, but one thing I can guarantee is that you'll never have the opportunity to verify that," Cara, the radio station rep, jumped in. Turning dark brown eyes to Kat, she explained. "Erik's known for his wild escapades…," she cocked her head to the side and rolled her eyes toward Seth, "…with the ladies."

Her words had been directed at Seth, but they'd settled in Kat's gut like a heavy weight. The night she met Erik, she'd suspected one-night stands were a way of life for him. That had been part of the reason she'd left while he was still sleeping. However, knowing it intuitively was a lot different than hearing about his sexcapades first hand.

Cut the crap, Kat.

Jealousy was ridiculous and immature. She'd been lucky enough to have one night with Erik, and the memories were hers forever. Tonight, however, was not the time to stroll down memory lane. The situation was surreal and like bad déjà vu. What would happen to her job if anyone found out she'd slept with Erik?

It was before you took this job—relax.

Easy to think, but hard to do with the past rushing at her like an out of control freight train destined for a horrible, fiery crash. She refused to let another promotion slip away because of a lapse in judgment. He'd been pissed off by her presence, so maybe he'd be happy to keep their fling quiet.

Tightness filled her chest at the thought of asking him to treat their night together as a dirty little secret. She was sure to him it had just been another one-night stand, but to her it had been more. Much more.

"His nickname is 'The Full Monty,'" Cara said, interrupting Kat's thoughts. "No one works harder than Erik, but he plays equally hard. He's wild and untamed. Many have tried, but most believe he'll never settle down."

Kat studied Cara as she absently stroked her arm and glanced around the room, obviously searching for the object of their discussion. Kat didn't know if she was being warned off Erik for her protection, or because Cara had designs on Erik and wanted one less competitor in the field. Either way, it didn't matter. Erik was off-limits to Kat regardless of his settling-down tendencies.

"You said the name of his company is Monteague Boats?" Kat asked.

Maggie confirmed with a nod of her head, and Kat ran a quick mental scan of the client list Rusty had passed on to her. She'd known Erik's last name and that he lived somewhere along the North Carolina coast. Although his name hadn't been the main focus of her memories, she felt certain if she'd stumbled across it on her client list, she would've noticed.

At least she could take small consolation in knowing that, even though he was a client of the agency, he wasn't one of her personal clients. Therefore, she wouldn't have to see him on a regular basis. He might even be a client who preferred doing everything via email and fax, and she wouldn't have to see him at all.

Feeling slightly better about the situation, she thanked the trio for their information and excused herself. After that near freak-out, she needed to slip into the backyard garden for some fresh air and a moment of solitude before diving back into the fray.

Chapter Two

T
he old Victorian's backyard garden was spectacular. The massive branches of the ancient oak trees were like giant arms, wrapping themselves protectively around the Victorian and all who resided within. Three magnolias stood sentry, protecting the side and back, while a climbing rose hung tenaciously to a trellis at the corner of the house. The fact that renovations had been completed without disturbing or destroying the rosebush, was a testament to the care and commitment Rusty had to restoring the old house to its original splendor.

Gardenias, azaleas, and jasmine wore the last few fading blooms of spring, while other plants were just beginning to stick their heads through the soil and wake from their winter slumber.

In the three days she'd been with SMG, she'd found the garden to be a peaceful refuge where she could grab a quick breath of fresh air or eat a quiet, leisurely lunch. The warm, homey atmosphere of the old Victorian, overlooking the Pamlico River from the front and surrounded by the peaceful gardens in the back, was the polar opposite to the chrome and glass environment of her old office. Everything about SMG implied the dog-eat-dog world of advertising might be a little gentler and friendlier in this small town.

She wound her way along the path, moving deeper into the garden oasis until she reached her favorite spot, the gazebo and Koi pond. She climbed the steps and stared into the water, watching the colorful gold, white, and brown spots flit back and forth while she tried to make sense of the past half hour.

Compartmentalizing had always been the key to maintaining her sanity, but as she sorted the information she'd just gathered into two separate compartments, personal and business, it kept collapsing back into one large debris pile: Erik.

He wasn't only a potential threat to her career; he was lethal to her emotional wellbeing. The universe had an incredibly warped sense of humor, and right now, it had to be getting one hell of a belly laugh at her expense. After the wildly tempestuous night she'd spent with him, no other man could turn her head. Now, when she needed to be fully focused on her job, who should appear but the physical incarnation of wild abandon himself?

"He's not Superman. He's just a normal, ordinary guy." Convincing the fish seemed easy enough. But the second she closed her eyes, memories from their night together crashed down on her, reminding her there was nothing ordinary about Erik Monteague.

She'd loved the feel of his long, muscular legs, covered by coarse, dark hair rubbing against her smooth ones. Then there was his butt... perfect for sinking her fingers into with each thrust. And that wasn't even his best feature. She groaned. He'd been nothing short of glorious stepping out of his boxers, stroking his—

"Here. You look like you could use this."

At the sound of Erik's voice, Kat's heart slammed into the front wall of her chest. She whipped around to face him, feeling like a child caught with her hand in the cookie jar—or her mind in his pants, as the case may be. As sweat popped out on her lip and the back of her neck, she prayed the accompanying blush couldn't be seen in the evening's dim light.

She flicked her gaze to his outstretched hand and the full-to-the-brim shot glass he offered. Needing to be a consummate professional, she'd kept her distance from the bar. But on the verge of snapping, that shot glass might be the only thing that kept her from swimming with the fish... so to speak.

"What is it?" she asked, reaching for the glass, silently cursing the shake that sent the liquid sloshing onto her hand.

"Southern Comfort with lime. Isn't that your preferred poison?" The ferocious scowl was gone and an intimate smile softened his face.

He remembered her drink preference?

She almost preferred the scowl because this look caused a warm, mushy feeling to stir low in her belly, which in turn, caused red flashing lights and warning bells to fire in her brain. Her life had no room for warm fuzzies right now, especially where he was concerned.

She closed her eyes and tossed the shot back like a pro. The heat sliding down her throat swirled with the warmth already building in her gut. She looked at the glass and considered the merits of rolling her tongue around the inside, hoping to maximize the benefits of every last drop.

However, being the mature adult she was, she settled for licking the remnants from her lips… a move Erik noticed.

She pulled her gaze away from his face and the heat in his eyes and began a quick body scan. Topsiders covered his sockless feet, which were braced shoulder width apart as if prepared for battle. Khaki pants did a good job of hiding the goods, but they didn't prevent her mind's eye from envisioning the thick cock and heavy sac that lay beneath the cotton fabric. A casual knit T-shirt stretched snugly across his stomach, broad chest, and shoulders.

His hand was tucked casually in his pocket and an amused smiled played on his lips, but his blue eyes weren't twinkling like they had the night they'd met. Instead, they were guarded, and his overall posture was stiff and cautious.

"Thanks," she said, holding up the shot glass before setting it on the gazebo railing. As if she hadn't already gotten the scoop on Erik and his association with SMG, she said, "What are you doing here?"

"Bringing you a drink. I recognized the signs of distress. Wide eyes, choking"—he glanced to her hand—"shaking hands. All good indicators of someone who needs a drink." He slipped his free hand into his pocket and shrugged. "I obliged."

Kat laughed nervously and crossed her arms over her stomach, trying to establish a barrier, even an inconsequential one, between them. "I meant what are you doing at SMG's open house."

"Rusty helps me handle the marketing for our company." Erik shifted his stance and in the process, moved a step closer. "What are you doing here?"

She straightened her shoulders and stood taller against his penetrating gaze, which seemed to search her face for more than just an answer to his question. "I'm working here as an account executive."

His expression softened. "I guess things didn't work out at your old job."

"It was for the best," she said, waving a hand in the air while trying to summon a nonchalant shrug. "I knew it wasn't going to change, so I started looking for another job pretty much right away. My non-compete agreement made things difficult." She laughed. "As it was designed to do, so it took me a while to find something I could accept."

Somewhere in the back of her mind, she had the awareness she should feel some kind of embarrassment standing here talking to him like this. She'd done things with this man she couldn't conceive of doing with anyone else, and yet she wasn't the slightest bit uncomfortable. The only thing she felt was an overwhelming desire to do it all again.

He moved another step closer.

She inched backwards and gripped the railing of the gazebo.

"When did you move here?"

"Last weekend. It's been a real whirlwind couple of weeks. I wanted to be here for the open house so I could meet as many clients as possible. I found a place to live, packed, and moved in a week's time." Dammit, she was rambling. Wide open silences always made her tense, so she tended to fill them with yammering. Which then made her more uptight.

And that was without him taking another step closer. "Where are you staying?"

She'd moved as far away as the railing would allow, so she tried her best not to breathe. When she inhaled she drew in the scent of his spicy cologne, one that perfectly complemented his spicy personality. But his scent, along with his looming presence and the heat radiating from his body, sizzled her brain.

"Uhhh…" She forced herself to focus on his question. "A few blocks from here. I've moved into an apartment over the old fire station. It has an incredible view of the river and town. I was lucky to find it."

"I saw a U-Haul and two guys moving furniture in last weekend."

"That was me."

His eyes narrowed. "Did someone come with you, or did you move alone?"

His tone carried the tiniest hint of jealousy, and she pressed her lips together to keep from smiling. She was being petty and childish, especially since a relationship with him was out of the question. But she could live with her juvenile joy. "Just me. A couple friends from Charlotte helped."

Taking one last step toward her, he stood so close they might be breaking public decency laws. In a low, menacing voice, he asked, "How good a friend?"

She managed to hold back her laughter, but a huge smile broke through. "A friend's fiancé and his brother."

He rested one forearm on the column above her head, placed his other hand on the railing next to her hip, and shifted his body so he effectively trapped her. "Why did you leave me like that?"

She gasped and her stomach tightened at his angry tone. She knew from their night together he was abrupt and direct, but she hadn't expected him to make the jump to something this personal so quickly.

His eyes were cold, his facial muscles tense, and the uncertainty she'd sensed in him earlier was back.

She chewed on her bottom lip and looked into his eyes. Much like the night they met, he compelled her in such a way she found it impossible to deny him anything, especially the truth. "I had no experience with one-night stands."

She swallowed the ugly taste in her mouth as she acknowledged what they'd shared as nothing more than inconsequential, meaningless sex. "I didn't know proper protocol. I thought I was doing the right thing by leaving and avoiding the awkward morning-after thing I've always heard about." Especially since she'd fallen head over heels for him in the span of twelve hours.

Erik's eyes flashed with what appeared to be anger, and he leaned down close to her ear. In a low, bone-melting drawl, he asked, "What made you so sure it was only gonna be one night?"

Her heart stopped momentarily, then picked up a pounding rhythm. "Wouldn't it have been?"

"Not as far as I was concerned. But since I had no way of finding you, you took that option away from me." He drew back slightly and shifted his gaze away. "I've gone back to that bar every time I've been in Charlotte, hoping to run into you again."

He stood too close, making it difficult to think clearly. She opened and closed her mouth a couple of times, but no words came out. He made it sound as if they might have had something more, if only she'd stuck around and given them a chance. But everything he said that night led her to believe he didn't do relationships. And what she heard tonight confirmed it.

But how many nights over the past thirteen months had she lain in bed, staring at the ceiling, wondering *what if?*

The muscle in his jaw tightened and flexed, and her fingers ached with the desire to reach out and caress the tic away. Moisture pooled in her mouth as she dropped her gaze to his neck. Would he taste salty if she slid her tongue over his pulse point?

Her breath became ragged as she struggled with the overwhelming need to launch herself against the massive wall of his body, throw her arms around his slender waist, and feel his arms wrapping her in a tender hug as she rested her head against his shoulder.

But instead of doing any of those things, she clenched her fists to her sides, ducked out from under his arms, and squeezed her eyes closed. No way in hell would she allow the tears prickling the backs of her eyes to fall. Once she'd regained her self-control, she turned to face him.

He'd propped his hip against the railing and crossed his arms over his chest. His eyes were filled with unasked questions.

"Erik, I'm sorry." She risked taking a step closer and searched his face for understanding. "I didn't know. I assumed... well... that the whole thing meant nothing to you." She ignored his flash of anger and continued. "I thought I was doing you a favor by being gone when you woke." She glanced away from his hardened gaze. "I came back. But when you didn't answer the door, I knew I'd done the right thing by leaving."

He jerked upright and grasped the railing in a tight grip. "What do you mean you came back?"

"After I left, I sat in my car for about twenty minutes arguing with myself, questioning if I'd done the right thing. I finally gave up and went back to your room. But when I knocked, you didn't answer." She shrugged as if wasn't a big deal. As if her heart hadn't cracked at the silence that met her.

He closed his eyes and cursed under his breath. When he opened them again they were shimmering with kindness and his entire demeanor had softened. "When you left, the click of the door woke me. I grabbed my pants to come after you, but the elevator doors were just shutting behind you. I paced around the room for a few minutes and finally decided..." He exhaled and shook his head. "Hell, I let pride get in the way." He brushed his knuckles across her cheek. "I don't chase after women, no matter how beautiful and sexy they are." He dropped his hand to his side. "You must have come back while I was in the shower, and I didn't hear you."

Kat stared at him in shock as an expanding hollowness filled her chest.

He caught her chin in his fingers and smiled. "But you're here now."

"Nothing can happen now." Her voice was a high-pitched wail.

"Why not?"

"Because," she threw her arms up in frustration, "I can't be involved with a client."

His mouth lifted and the corners of his eyes crinkled. "There are varying degrees of involvement."

"Erik, I'm serious. My involvement with a client cost me my last job. I'll never make that mistake again."

Completely unfazed, he persisted. "Never say never, Kat. Besides, I'm not asking for a long-term commitment, just a few dates." His smooth, rich voice heated her from the inside out, and the way he stroked his fingers along her cheek as he spoke was hypnotizing. "We can work on discovering a few more of those erogenous zones. C'mon, don't tell me you're not interested in finding a few more hot buttons."

Of course she was interested. What living, breathing female wouldn't be? But she couldn't. She wouldn't. Not when her job was on the line. Again.

Resolve firmly in place, she squared her shoulders and lifted her chin. "No, Erik. I'm sorry, I can't."

And before she shed her resolve, and her clothes, in favor of more frenzied sex with the hottest man she'd ever met, she turned away from him and all but ran toward the safety of the office door.

As she rounded a magnolia, she heard him say, "We'll see about that."

***

"Dammit," Kat growled as she threw her pencil on the desk, then ground her palms into her eyeballs. Trying to proofread technical data sheets before they went to press was tedious on a good day. The type was small, the words were boring, and reading something this detailed required a tremendous amount of focus—something she couldn't find anywhere.

She had her requisite Diet Coke, plus one; nibbled her way through a chocolate bar, king size; and gotten up to stretch, several times. All to no avail.

Sexual frustration had become an all-consuming state, permeating every cell of her persistently aroused body and crawling into the deepest, darkest recesses of her mind. She hadn't had sex with anyone since Erik and, surprisingly, she hadn't even missed it. Since seeing him, however, she couldn't seem to think about anything but sex. Specifically, sex with him.

During the day, she struggled to focus on work. At night, her subconscious took over and held her hostage. The dreams were erotic. The details, vivid. The sex, intense. And she always awoke aroused and aching.

But last night's dream had been different, and she couldn't shake free from the memory, or the feelings it inspired. Rather than a fast and furious get-your-rocks-off fucking pace, the sex had been slow and leisurely. It had been passionate, sweet lovemaking with a complete fusion of their bodies and souls. Never having experienced anything like it in the flesh, the dream left her emotionally raw.

She rested her head against the back of the chair and stared at the stark-white ceiling. No woman with enough breath in her to fog a mirror could resist Erik Monteague or the intense chemistry between them. If simply seeing him created this many problems for her, she couldn't imagine how bad it would be had she been forced to work with him. The hormonal stress would've killed her.

She took a deep breath, released it on an "oohhmmm," and leaned back over the data sheets, determined to get this job finished. She'd just found her place when Rusty stuck his head into her office. "Hey, Kat, got a minute?"

After another silent *Ooohhhmmm*, she said, "Sure, what's up?"

With one hand in his pocket and a thick manila folder tucked under his arm, Rusty strolled across her office. He drew his free hand down his jawline, then massaged the muscles at the back of his neck. "This new business project I'm working on is monopolizing my time. I'm confident we're going to pick it up, so in fairness to our current clients, I think I need to turn over several of my accounts. I've given Elise two, the jewelry store and the Chamber projects." He sat in the chair across from Kat's desk, rested an ankle on his knee, and tossed the folder onto her desk. "But you'll be a much better fit for this one."

Kat took a quick look at the name on the folder and stopped breathing. This had to be a joke. No way in hell was he actually passing the Monteague Boats account over to her.

But why would he joke about something like this? He didn't know about her and Erik's history—at least she hoped he didn't—and guys didn't do shit like this to tease.

She forced air into her lungs and smiled. "Okay. I'll look over the file, familiarize myself with the account"—*freak out*—"and give them a call. Is there anything pressing I should know about? Any upcoming deadlines?"

Rusty's sheepish look caused the king-sized candy bar and soda to gurgle in her gut. "Erik Monteague is the contact person. He's head of the marketing department as well as one of the owners. And, he'll be here in thirty minutes for a meeting."

Thirty minutes! She jerked upright and forced the air to keep moving through her lungs… in, out, in, out. "Wow," she said, forcing a small laugh. "It's a good thing I'm a quick study."

She made a quick mental to-do list—thirty minutes to go over their entire advertising history, see what ads they were currently running, get a feel for their past campaigns, and most importantly, squash out the slut brigade (aka hormones) and their recently launched sexual offensive.

She was good at her job, and the first three would be easy. The fourth was questionable. She'd come to realize over the past several days that the slut brigade was a formidable foe.

"When Erik gets here, I'll make the introductions and get you started." He stood and headed for the door, then paused. "I think you and Erik will work well together; it'll be a good fit."

Yeah, that's the problem. Erik and I are a perfect *fit.*

After closing the door for privacy, Kat stared out the window at the park and boardwalk across the street and the expansive Pamlico River beyond it. She was quickly coming to appreciate the river and the calming effect it had on her. Since her backyard oasis had been tainted—she'd never eat there again without smelling Erik's scent or remembering the way his heat had surrounded her—the park would make a great substitute refuge.

Several moms pushed strollers along the boardwalk and watched their children play in the park. A toddler snagged Kat's attention as he threw pellets of food in the air, then jumped up and down, clapping his hands as seagulls swooped in to catch the offering. Even at this distance, his delight was contagious and Kat felt herself begin to smile.

Dark, unruly hair whipped around his head as he ran back to his mother for more food and Kat found herself thinking, *That's what Erik would've looked like at that age.*

Dammit. Her shoulders slumped as she thunked her forehead against the cool glass of the window. She had to stop picturing Erik in every scenario. She'd done it to a small degree before seeing him at the party last Thursday night, but it was quickly growing into a habit and a constant source of irritation, like wet sand in a bathing suit.

She turned from the window and glared at the offensive folder on her desk, thinking back to the night she'd met Erik, when she'd been drowning in a pathetic sea of failure. Would he question her ability to handle his account?

No, he seemed like a fair and reasonable person, and she didn't believe that would be a concern of his unless she gave him reason, which meant she needed to put her personal feelings aside and go into that meeting prepared and focused. She was a professional, dammit, and it was time to pull herself together and act like one.

Chapter Three

As Erik pulled his boat into a slip at Riverside's public marina, he couldn't wipe the stupid-ass grin off his face. The sky was Carolina blue with a few puffy clouds. A light breeze pushed small ripples across the water, and the temperature and humidity were low. It was a perfect spring day.

He tied off the boat, then gave his best four-legged friend, Little Bit, the command to stay, before making his way down the dock to the park. Of all the places he could've been born, Erik was tremendously grateful he'd been plopped down in this little coastal haven.

Although renovations had recently been completed to improve the boardwalk and waterfront park, the town remained much as it had been for the past two hundred years. As he made his way across the park toward SMG, he considered the love-hate relationship the town had with the great Pamlico River. The river served as a lifeline to many of Riverside's residents, and prior to becoming industrialized, it had been necessary for the town's survival.

But a hurricane could turn the river into an angry and violent monster that destroyed everything in its path. The relationship between the town and the river was like a relationship between two people. When things were working, it was a beautiful thing. When they weren't, it could mean total devastation.

Something he'd be well served to remember as he damn near skipped across the street to SMG and Kat. Keeping things in perspective was going to be crucial.

Since his night with Kat, he'd gone out a few times, but he always found himself unfairly comparing each woman to her, and the dates ultimately imploded. Meeting with Kat would give him the perfect opportunity to charm her into agreeing to pick up where they'd left off, so they could enjoy a few wild romps, and he could get her out of his system once and for all. Afterwards, they could continue on as friends, and he could get back to his regularly scheduled programming.

The self-preservationist—the part of his mind he normally always listened to—waved his arms and sent out warning flares at Erik's poor planning and faulty thinking.

It seemed to believe any involvement with Kat would end up about as serious as a man could get, but Erik held firm to the notion he was simply in it for sex. What was the worst thing that could happen, an orgasm overdose?

For the first time in ten years, Erik chose to ignore the self-preservationist and slammed the door shut on that part of his mind.

As he pushed through the front door of SMG, Luanna, the young, perky receptionist, smiled broadly. "Good morning, Erik. Here to see Rusty?"

The stupid grin he'd been wearing since receiving Rusty's phone call widened. "I don't know about Rusty, but I'm definitely meeting with Kat."

While Luanna rang Kat and double-checked with Rusty about his participation, Erik relaxed in one of the lobby chairs. He was staring at the floor, lost in thought, when a pair of three-inch heels crossed his field of vision.

Lord have mercy.

He took a deep breath and oh so slowly raked his gaze up the pair of long legs he knew fit so nicely around his waist. Rusty's pounding footsteps on the balcony above and his quick appearance on the stairs halted Erik's visual meandering at the hemline of her short black skirt.

"Hey, man, how's it going?" Rusty called out as he descended the steps.

Up was the first thing that came to Erik's mind as he stood and shook hands with Rusty. However, despite his raunchy reputation, he wasn't that crass, so he responded in an appropriate manner. "Great." Releasing Rusty's grip, he turned to Kat and smiled. "How are you this mornin'?"

She clutched a file folder to her chest with her left hand while offering her right for a shake. Her smile was tight, her demeanor stiff, obviously not as happy about this meeting as him. "I'm good. Thanks for asking. And you?"

When he extended his hand, she gave him more of a slap than a shake, and he bit the inside of his cheek to keep from laughing. No prolonged touching on her part... He'd enjoy working to change that.

"I'm fantastic, and I'm looking forward to this." He knew she caught his subtle innuendo by the spark of irritation in her eyes. Rusty had turned his back, so Erik winked and motioned for her to precede him into the conference room.

"Did the two of you have a chance to meet at the open house?" Rusty asked.

Before Kat could reply, Erik said, "Oh yeah. We've met."

Kat's eyes widened in alarm and panic crossed her face as she pulled out a chair and took a seat.

Rusty had his back to Kat and Erik, digging through one of the conference room's built-in cabinets. "Great. That makes this even easier. I thought I'd get you guys started, then let her take over."

Erik gave Kat a nefarious smile and took a seat directly across from her. "Sounds good."

Rusty gave up his search and turned to face them. "I thought I had the Monteague portfolio in here, but I guess it's in my office." Moving around the end of the table toward the door, he glanced to Erik. "Kat's a skilled account executive and will be a great addition to your team."

Kat cleared her throat and shifted in her seat as a cute pink colored her neck and cheeks. Glancing to the notepad in front of her, she said, "I'm sure Erik has a full schedule. Why don't we go ahead and get started?"

Erik leaned back in his chair, crossed his legs at the ankles, and laced his hands over his stomach. "I'm ready."

His relaxed demeanor was the exact opposite of Kat's, and when she noticed Rusty exiting the room, her eyes widened. "Aren't you joining us?"

He paused and turned. "No. I need to get some things ready for an afternoon meeting. I just wanted to make introductions if you hadn't already met." He shifted his attention to Erik. "I've got the utmost confidence in Kat. She'll take good care of you."

Erik let the smile pushing at his mouth break through, and said, "I have no doubt she will. I'm looking forward to it."

Looking slightly shell-shocked and definitely rattled, Kat began taking slow, even breaths. Her transformation was fascinating, and more than a little disconcerting, to watch. It was as if each breath altered a part of her, causing the human Kat to melt away and a cool, distant robotic version to appear.

When the transformation was complete, she said, "I've gone over your past campaigns…"

He saw her mouth moving, but he was so off balance by the whole I-am-Zen routine, he wasn't able to follow the monotone words coming out of her tight lips. In order to rein in her control that quickly, she'd had to use the same technique many, many times.

"…target audience and objective…"

Was it a defense mechanism she'd developed to control her emotions after things had gone down the shitter at her last job, or had she been doing this for years?

"…positioning in the marketplace…"

Whatever her reasons, he didn't like this cold, non-human version of Kat. He wanted his Kat back.

Wait… what? What in the fucking hell was this "his Kat" shit?

With his mind bouncing around like a pinball, it took him a minute to realize she was staring at him, waiting for a response to her recitation. "Did I use too many big words and confuse you?"

He started to smile at the crack, but then, realizing she'd made a small joke, she pressed her lips together and took another deep breath.

Jesus, this was absurd. It was time for him to do a little cracking of his own to see if he could find the old Kat again. "No, I'm with you. Go ahead."

"Okay, let's talk about your target."

Erik tilted his head to the side and met her gaze head on. "I thought I'd made that clear the other night. You're my target."

She sucked in a quick breath and glanced at the conference room's open door before grabbing her pen and scratching notes. "Target… boat buyers." Keeping her gaze on the paper in front of her, she said, "Okay, let's talk about your objectives. Obviously, to sell more boats—"

"That's one of them. But it's certainly not the one I'm thinking about at the moment."

At his suggestive tone, she gripped the pen so tightly he could almost hear the thing squeal in pain. He figured the notes being etched into the paper this time had to do with personal directives of where he could go, rather than the direction of his business. Damn, it was so wrong to yank her chain this way, but the more annoyed she got, the hotter he got.

After another deep breath, she said, "Okay, let's talk about positioning."

Seeing this as his homerun opportunity, he waited to answer until she glanced at him to verify he'd heard the question. When she did, he locked gazes with her and allowed every ounce of desire pumping through his veins to show. "Positioning?" He rested his forearms on the table and leaned toward her. "I would love to talk positioning with you. Better yet, how about I show you?"

The pulse in her neck fluttered and her breathing grew choppy. He felt guilty for pushing her like this when she was so obviously uncomfortable around him, but he couldn't stop. It was rare to find someone who matched his intensity—both in and out of the bedroom—and he wanted to break through this damned shell she'd created and see that fire again.

The fact that he wanted to see it outside the realm of sex should have been another warning flag, but fuck it, heeding warnings didn't seem to top his priority list today.

Leaning back from the table to give the illusion of more space between them, he said, "Why don't you come with me to the plant? You can see how things work firsthand, see the finished product."

Kat's eyes widened. "I—"

"That's a great idea."

In unison, Kat and Erik whipped their head to Rusty as he swung through the conference room door. Gesturing to the portfolio tucked under his arm, he said, "This has all the old brochures and magazine ads. But pictures in brochures don't do justice to Erik's operation. Do you have anything else scheduled this morning?"

Panic flashed in Kat's eyes, but that fucking mask dropped right back into place, quickly concealing her emotions.

Before she could voice the protests he knew was coming, Erik said, "Better yet… you probably wouldn't be comfortable walking around the plant in your suit and high heels." But he so wanted to see her in those heels… and nothing else… later. "Why don't we go this afternoon? That way you can change into more comfortable clothes."

Translated: *That way you won't be able to use work as an excuse to rush back, and maybe I can convince you to have dinner with me.*

"That's even better," Rusty said as he dumped the portfolio on the conference room table, then stuck his fist out to Erik for a knuckle bump. "Erik, good to see you."

As Rusty hustled out of the conference room, Kat dropped her head onto crossed arms on the table. The heaving of her shoulders let him know she was back to the heavy breathing, but he had the feeling this time she was thinking *I'm-so-pissed* rather than *I-am-Zen*.

He stood and made his way around the table, then wrapped his fingers over her shoulders and began massaging the tension out of them. Leaning over, he whispered in her ear, "Does three o'clock work for you?"

She lifted her head and muttered, "Like it matters if it does or not."

Only an idiot would laugh, so he bit his lip and, sounding as sincere as possible, said, "Of course it matters. Is three-thirty better?"

He wasn't certain, but he thought she mumbled "bastard" along with "Three is fine."

***

Kat stopped dead in her tracks on the marina catwalk and stared in disbelief. "What the hell is that?"

Erik tried to look innocent, but it was a wasted attempt. She'd bet he couldn't squeeze an ounce of innocence from his entire body. "It's my boat."

She ignored the obvious and focused on the creature sitting on the bow of the boat. The one with the wagging tail and tongue flopping out of the corner of its mouth. "What's that thing *on* the boat?"

"Little Bit."

She narrowed her eyes and leaned in for a closer look. "Little bit of what?"

Erik laughed as he knelt and rubbed the creature's head. "They said at the pound he was a little bit of everything, so that's what I named him. Little Bit."

"You have a dog?"

He twisted his head around to look at her. "Why does that shock you?"

"Because... well... that makes you... domesticated."

"What?" Amusement crinkled his face, but his tone was guarded.

"Yeah, and getting him from the pound is nice."

He stood and turned to face her. "You don't think I'm nice?"

"No."

He cocked his head to the side and all traces of amusement melted away.

"No! I mean, oh, hell." She rubbed her hand across her forehead and took a deep breath. "It's just that getting him from the pound is a nice-guy move. I need you to keep being a jerk."

"That night at dinner, you mentioned volunteering at the animal shelter. You said there were tons of animals there that needed good homes."

He remembered that?

"When Steve started talking about getting a dog, I told him to check it out. I went with him, and as soon as I saw LB, I knew I had to have him." He glanced at the dog and smiled affectionately. "He's so u-g-l-y, I was afraid no one else would adopt him."

Her mouth dropped open. "Did you just spell ugly so you wouldn't hurt the dog's feelings?"

He smiled shyly and lifted a shoulder. "He's pretty smart."

She slid her gaze to the brown, black, and white dog with a long snout, ears that stood straight up, and a long, slender body. He was ugly. But he was also kind of cute… in an ugly sort of way. And, based on the way his big, brown eyes tracked every move Erik made, he adored his master.

Damn, damn, damn. Not only did Erik get a dog from the shelter—one of the nicest things a person could do in her book—he got the ugly one. She barely managed to keep from stomping her foot as she harrumphed in frustration. Talk about unfair.

"And what do you mean 'keep being a jerk'?"

Her irritation had almost escaped, but she snatched it back like a lifeline. As long as she stayed angry, she could maintain her emotional distance. If she maintained her distance, she could keep this unconventional meeting focused on business. "Yeah, remember how you manipulated things this morning? That was being a jerk." She glanced around and said, "Why are we at the marina? It appears you expect me to get on that boat."

His grin was quick and fleeting. "By the time I drive ten miles up the south side of the river, cross the connector and bridge, then drive the eight miles back down this side, it takes me thirty minutes to get here from the plant. I can go from one side of the river to the other, by boat, in less than half that time. Plus, it's a beautiful day. Why not take advantage of it?"

"I'm supposed to be working." And this fell under the category of fun.

"You are working," Erik said, jumping on to the boat with practiced ease. "What better way to learn about boats than to ride on one?" He extended his hand. "Give me your hand, and I'll help you climb aboard."

She chewed her bottom lip and considered the wisdom of trying to "climb aboard" without his help. Accept his hand and suffer the cruel and unusual punishment of touching him for the second time today? Or—she glanced down her sundress to her sandals—make a go of it on her own and risk taking a swim?

"Take my hand, Kat. I won't bite." A seductive smile that mirrored his easy drawl slid across his lips. "Unless you want me to."

Unwilling to be outdone—or undone—by him, she ignored her curling toes and the warming in her belly and took his hand. His large, strong hand that completely enveloped hers. She silently cursed the universe for putting her in this position, knowing this brief encounter couldn't and wouldn't go any further than this one magnificent touch.

As she struggled to gracefully maneuver over the boat's railing, she asked, "Why didn't you tell me we were going on a boat? When you said 'wear something comfortable' I didn't know you meant a bathing suit and flip-flops." With both feet firmly planted on the boat's deck, she shook her hand free of his.

He took her laptop bag and purse and stashed them inside a hatch. "Would you have agreed to come with me if I'd told you?"

"I wouldn't have agreed to come with you, at all, if I hadn't felt forced."

The jerk had the audacity to smile. And not just any smile, but one capable of melting right through her armor. "Then I guess it's my lucky day." Reducing the wattage on the smile, he said, "I'm sorry for manipulating you. But I do think seeing the plant will help you get a better feel for our operation and the high quality boats we manufacture." He moved a step closer. "I'll make it up to you, if you'll let me."

Oh, no. Uh-uh… absolutely not. "Nope, no making up necessary."

He chuckled and gave her a can't-blame-a-guy-for-trying shrug. While Erik made quick work of untying the ropes and maneuvered them out of the marina, Little Bit did his impression of a hood ornament, standing on the bow with his nose in the air, ears flapping in the breeze.

They'd both done this so many times they had a routine, but Kat was lost. There weren't any seats at the front of the boat, and she wasn't about to sit on the bench seat with Erik at the steering console. There were two seats at the rear, but they seemed kind of low, and she wasn't sure how wet she'd get sitting back there. She glanced to Erik and shouted over the winding motor. "Where do you want me?"

The slow turn of his head, the wicked gleam in his eyes, and a smile that promised sex on the half shell said he could make *anywhere* work just fine.

At this crucial time in her life, she needed an army of angels sitting on her shoulders, prodding her toward good, responsible behavior. Instead, she had the slut brigade, and they weren't *prodding* her toward anything. They were propelling her, with a raging lust, toward bad, irresponsible, illicit behavior with six feet of wicked temptation.

But resist she must.

She threw up her hand to block the magnetic pull of the smile spreading across his glorious mouth. "You know what I meant. Where do you want me to sit?"

"What?" Again, with more of the wasted innocence. "I knew whatcha meant. And I was going to say that it's not rough, so you can sit or stand anywhere."

She chose a seat at the back and had just settled into the hypnotic rhythm of the boat when they came to an abrupt stop. Alarmed, she jerked upright in the seat. "What's wrong? Why'd you stop?"

Erik seemed to be smiling from the inside out as he pointed to something in the water on the left side of the boat.

She stood for a closer look just as a porpoise jumped out of the water. She gasped in surprise and ran to the railing. A second jumped and rolled, quickly followed by a third.

Erik left the boat idling in neutral and moved to the railing next to her. "I swear, I think they know the sound of my boat." His wide smile and the wonder in his voice clearly indicated he liked the recognition.

As the trio circled closer and closer, Erik leaned over the railing and let his fingers dangle in the water. One of the porpoises rolled onto its side and brushed against Erik's fingertips as it slipped under the boat. The second followed suit, while the third jumped and rolled, appearing to do tricks for their benefit.

"They swim past my house every night, but I thought we'd be too early to see them now."

Kat watched, awestruck, as the porpoises took turns brushing against Erik's hands. "Have you ever swum with them?"

His smile broadened. "Yeah, last summer. We were skiing and they kept circling us and wouldn't leave. We were afraid we'd end up hitting them, so we put the skis away and swam with them instead."

"I want to swim with them!" The announcement flew out of her mouth without any conscious thought. "Well, obviously not today, but…" She would love a carefree swim with these beautiful creatures someday.

Erik laughed as his gaze raked her from head to toe. "You could always go skinny dipping."

She playfully kicked off her shoes and grabbed the hem of her dress, pretending to take the suggestion. Laughing, and totally lost to the moment, she heard him murmur, "There's the Kat I knew."

He might as well have picked her up and dunked her head first into the cold water. What was she thinking? At the first sight of the porpoises, she'd chunked her professionalism into the river like an old, ratty bag. The old Kat had barreled through without a care in the world, and it had taken his comment—his subtle reminder of who she'd been the night they met—to snap her out of it.

Seeing her sudden change, Erik said, "Relax. You're too uptight. You need to let go a little."

She straightened her dress and slid her feet back into her sandals. Who was he to lecture her on how to behave? He didn't know anything about her… well, other than how much she liked that thing he did with his—

Stay on topic here, Kat.

Erik didn't know that, more than anything, she longed to "let go." But she couldn't afford to do that now—opportunities to prove she could be successful were dwindling.

She crossed her arms over her stomach and took a step back. "You know, maybe you should 'let go' a little less. It seems you have quite the reputation as a party-hard playboy." She refused to look at the ugly green-eyed monster making its appearance with that comment. She was on a roll, and she didn't have time to stop and make its acquaintance. "Maybe if you worked a little harder and partied a little less you wouldn't have lost that account in Charlotte."

She gasped, horrified. "Omigod!" She'd never spoken to a client in such a rash and hostile way. She threw her hand over her mouth, nearly in shock. "I can't believe I said that. I am so, so sorry."

Erik stood frozen, equally stunned by her outburst. Her fingers numbed, and heat exploded in her face and neck as he slowly crossed his arms and leaned a hip against the rail.

Breathing in short, rapid bursts, with her stomach knotted like a pretzel, she said, "Saying I'm sorry isn't nearly enough." She wanted to grab his arm and beg him to not be angry, but instead, she swallowed hard and gripped the railing with a sweaty palm. "I don't know where that came from. I'm sorry for being so out of line."

She held her breath and waited for blistering words to explode from his lips. Instead, he rested one hand on the railing and the other on his hip, before calmly saying, "At least we're getting somewhere." He chuckled. "Even if it is blatant hostility, it's nice to see that inner fire that drew me to you in the first place." His gaze softened. "What's happened to you, Kat? Where did you get the notion that you can't have fun?"

She exhaled and slumped against the center console. "All my life I've been criticized for having my head in the clouds. Being too spontaneous. Not taking life seriously enough. I've been told over and over and over I should be more like my brother." Sadness filled her chest as she watched the porpoises swim away… the perfect symbolism for her life at the moment. "I can't afford to play and have fun and mess up the opportunity to make VP." Emotion clogged her throat as she thought about her grandfather. He wasn't getting any younger, and she had to make him proud before he left her. "It's my last chance to prove that I'm not a total screw-up."

He took her chin in his fingers and turned her head so she was forced to look at him. Holding her gaze, he said, "You are not a screw-up. We've all made mistakes. You have to forgive yourself for what happened at your old job and move on." Shadows moved in his eyes and a pained expression crossed his features before he dropped his hand and turned away from her to face the water. "But most importantly, you have to keep being you."

She had the feeling something more besides her "uptightness" was bothering Erik, but he'd closed himself off to her and she couldn't get a bead on his emotions. Deciding to let it go and return the focus to her latest misstep, she said, "I'm good at my job. I'm sure you find that hard to believe, considering the circumstances under which we met and my recent outburst. But I swear to you, I am competent, and I'll never cross that line again."

"I believe you're more than competent. Rusty never would've hired you if you weren't, and he sure as hell wouldn't have turned my account over to you. As for that line…" He looked at her from the corner of his eye and smiled. "You're the hottest thing I've ever seen when you're all fired up—whether it comes from passion or anger doesn't matter. Personally, I hope to see you cross that line again and again and again."

Chapter Four

Ten minutes later, Erik laughed to himself as he eased the boat into his slip at Monteague's marina and wondered what Kat thought about designated boat slips at a place of employment. Antsy to get back on solid ground, Little Bit jumped and bounced around until Erik said, "Wait a minute, boy. You know the rule. Ladies first." LB flopped down and waited while Erik tied off the boat, then pulled Kat's bags from the hatch and set them on the pier's storage box.

After their talk, she returned to her seat and remained sullen and withdrawn. He figured she instituted a self-imposed timeout for her flare-up, and rather than continuing to push, he backed off and let her have her space.

He knew she was angry with herself, but he saw her comments as the defensive mechanism they were and didn't take them personally. No sane person could ever question his dedication or work ethic, not with the hours he put in. He also had the benefit of knowing his job performance hadn't had anything to do with losing that account in Charlotte. It didn't actually have anything to do with Monteague Boats at all. The dealer had been forced to reduce inventory, and Monteague had been a victim of circumstance.

Of course, Erik hadn't been happy about the loss of business. But when she'd met him in that bar, he hadn't been drinking away the loss of the account like he told her. It had nothing do with his job and everything to do with the date.

April fifth.

He'd spent nine years trying to figure out a way to get through that day. The first couple of years he tried the drunken-stupor approach. When that hadn't worked he tried working himself to the point of exhaustion, hoping to sleep the day away without even realizing it had come and gone. But nothing had made a difference.

Until Kat.

This year, when April fifth rolled around, he spent more time thinking about her than Lindsey. Part of him felt guilty as hell about it. A large part felt tremendous relief.

But the Kat standing at the back of the boat, with a sad smile and yearning look in her eyes, wasn't the same Kat he'd met that night. Then, even though she'd been upset about her job, she'd been full of life and had laughed until she cried, making him laugh right along with her. The amount of alcohol they consumed helped, but it certainly wasn't the biggest contributing factor... that had been Kat's fun-loving personality.

He'd caught breakthrough flashes of the old Kat in the gazebo and again today, but she was working so hard to suppress her carefree spirit, he had to wonder what had caused such a significant change in her. It didn't take a genius to see how unhappy she was.

What he struggled most to understand, though, was why it mattered to him. He was supposed to be seducing her, having a frenzied night or two (or three) of great sex, to work her out of his system, then moving on.

Nothing more. Nothing personal. And certainly no involvement.

And yet, looking at her now, he'd do anything to make her laugh and smile again. To make her happy.

He double-checked the ropes, helped her off the boat before following, then led her up the pier to the back door of Monteague's corporate offices. Once inside, he turned left, went halfway down the hall, then turned right into his office.

"I need to check voicemail. Can I get you something to drink while you wait?"

"No, thanks. I'm fine." She looked around the office, taking it all in, and he tried to see it as she might. Well-worn leather sofa—he couldn't begin to count the nights he'd slept there because he'd worked so late he didn't have the energy to go home. Coffee table in front of it covered with boating and fishing magazines. The wall to the right of the door housed a wet bar complete with mini fridge. His mahogany desk sat in front of a large picture window overlooking the Pamlico and was covered from one end to the other with boat plans, folders, and magazines. His office had operated much like a home over the years, and that contributed to its well-lived-in appearance.

While he retrieved his messages, he watched Kat gravitate to the wall decorated with plaques and recognition awards like a nail being drawn to a magnet. He always felt like that wall screamed, "Hey, look at me. Look what a great guy I am," and he hated it. He and the company didn't make charitable contributions because they wanted the recognition. They did it because they wanted to help the community. However, he always made sure to put the recognition plaques on display somewhere, because if he didn't, sure as shit, the person who gave it to him would drop by and notice it missing.

As he hung up the phone and rose from his chair, she turned awe-filled eyes to him. "This is amazing. Why didn't I see press releases for any of this?"

"We don't do any." Her mouth dropped open, and, knowing what was coming, he rushed to cut off her protest. "We don't do it for the recognition."

"Obviously. But you should take advantage of it. Let the community know how much you give back."

"No." Through the years, he and Rusty had gone ten rounds over the subject, but Erik felt strongly about it, and he wouldn't be dissuaded. "It's not up for discussion, so let's save ourselves the future hassle where this is concerned."

Hoping for a quick end to the debate, he walked to the door and gave her his special smile. The one he'd been perfecting since he was a little boy and realized its magical power. "You ready for the tour?"

***

Two hours later, Kat walked down the pier toward the boat, her head a congested traffic jam of thoughts. Erik and Rusty had been right. Pictures didn't do justice to Monteague's impressive state-of-the-art facility. However, that wasn't what had left her dizzy.

When she'd left work this afternoon, her goal had been to go with Erik, see their manufacturing plant, and get a clear understanding of the boat-building process. What she hadn't considered was the personal insight she would glean into Erik. Seeing him in his work environment and watching him interact with the employees and his father had completely changed the playing field. A part of her brain was suggesting the rules, and maybe even the game itself, had just been seriously altered.

Erik extended his hand to help her on board, and this time, rather than fighting it, she accepted without hesitation. She even allowed herself to enjoy the rush of heat accompanying the touch. Once she was settled, he scooped Little Bit into his arms and climbed aboard behind her.

Untying the ropes, he said, "Well, what do think?"

Having spent the past several hours with Erik, who had the innate ability to relax everyone around him, she didn't have it in her to be snide or defensive. "You were right. You have a tremendous facility. I had no idea boat building was so advanced and high tech. You should be proud of the business your family has built."

He snapped his head around to face her with a shocked expression on his face. Slowly recovering from his surprise, a smile spread over his mouth. "Thanks. That means a lot."

In a less hostile mood than she'd been when they crossed the river the first time, she took her seat in the back and looked around as he eased out of the slip. The sun was low in the sky and glittered off the surface of the water like a million shards of white, orange, and pink glass. The river was wide with tributaries snaking out in all directions. *Where do they all go?* she wondered.

She relaxed with the rocking of the boat as it sliced through the water and allowed its peaceful, calming effects to wash over her. Resting her head against the seat, she closed her eyes and enjoyed the sun's warming rays, while the cool breeze brushed across her skin.

As usual, anytime she closed her eyes and relaxed, thoughts of Erik took over. This time, rather than fighting the images dancing in front of her mind's eye, she let them roll. The man was an enigma she found unsettling and frightening. Sure, she'd spent an evening with him, drinking and laughing in the bar, then having an intimate dinner before the debauchery started. But that time together had been superficial and, for all she knew, could've been an act on his part.

But the last two hours… that was the real deal.

And it scared the hell out of her.

He might be the head of marketing, but he was an authority on every aspect of their business. He'd explained the entire process to her, step by step and in great detail. And he'd done so with the enthusiasm of a man who had a true passion for his job. He obviously worked hard, but he didn't seem resentful. Instead, he embraced it.

Several times throughout the tour he'd been hands on, like when he climbed onto a large boat and helped the electrician solve a wiring problem. When they reached the grinding booth, where they cut the holes for windows and hatches, he'd waited for the grinder to finish his current job so he could speak with him.

From the bits and pieces she overheard, she gathered the man's daughter was sick and had been for a while. Erik told him the company would take care of the medical bills not covered by insurance so the family wouldn't have that stress and could focus on her care.

The man's relief had been tremendous. Just thinking about the way the stress lines had eased from his eyes and forehead as he grabbed Erik's hand and thanked him profusely made her a little emotional all over again.

Erik spoke to everyone with kindness, and it was obvious the employees respected and admired him. The only time she'd noticed any tension in him was when his father mentioned an upcoming dinner Erik needed to attend. He'd muttered something about rigging up his keg, then assured his father he'd be there.

He was confident and self-assured. He laughed a lot, was playful and sexier than any man had a right to be. And his smile. Lord, his smile was infectious and heated her blood to the point of boiling. It had been her undoing the night they met, and she suspected, if he worked at it even a little bit, it would still be her undoing.

She thought back to the night they met and how he looked sitting at that bar with his head hung over his glass. His tortured expression matched hers, and she knew he'd also lost something important. She flopped onto the bar stool next to him and offered to buy his next drink. She hadn't done it to pick him up. She just wanted the company and thought maybe he could use a little himself. But then he laughed and smiled.

And she melted.

Then came the rest of the night. God, the way he whispered in her ear, telling her all the things he planned to do right before actually doing them, still got her hot. She licked her dry lips, trying to restore the moisture that had evacuated to a more favorable spot further south. She squeezed her thighs together, attempting to assuage the throb beginning to build.

Warm air swept across her neck, and she flung her eyes open. She'd been so caught up in her memories, she hadn't noticed the boat stopping, or that they were drifting in the middle of the river.

Palms planted on either side of her seat, Erik leaned over her wearing the expression of someone about to have lunch. "What's going on it that pretty head of yours?" His voice was a soft, cajoling rumble, but his eyes were hot and devouring.

She glanced down at her erect nipples pushing through the fabric of her sundress. Her knees were clenched, her hand caught between them where she'd been rubbing her inner thighs.

His mouth hovered inches above hers, and the need to grab the front of his shirt, pull him to her, lick his full bottom lip, and kiss him senseless was uncontrollable. The pungent scent of aftershave and hot man drifted over her, while the heat of his body wrapped around her like a cloak, drawing her to him. Her body lifted and drifted toward him of its own free will.

She shouldn't do this.

She couldn't stop.

Suddenly, something cold brushed against the heated skin of her leg. She jumped and looked down at Little Bit, who was nudging his way in between her and Erik. He looked expectantly from her to Erik, then back to her again and nudged her leg with his cold nose. He seemed to be saying, "There's some petting happening here, and I want my share."

Laughing nervously, she sank back down into her seat and rubbed her damp palm across the top of LB's head. He didn't seem to mind being used as a napkin, so she kept at it and said, "How long until we're back at the office?"

Erik, who had been completely undeterred by Little Bit's efforts, kept his hot and inviting gaze locked onto her. "Depends on what you have in mind once we get there. With the right incentive, I could get us there pretty damn quick." He straightened and looked around. "Or, we could take a little detour." The corner of his mouth lifted. "I know a great private spot off the creek over there."

"I bet you do." She rubbed her temples and sighed. God, she'd wanted to kiss him, and she hadn't wanted to stop at a kiss. But she was grateful for the intervention. She had to be strong and resist. She couldn't risk involvement with a client again. "No, no detours. I need to get back to the office."

"Could I talk you into having dinner with me?"

"I wish I could, but I can't." Gah, she was so torn. Despite the lecture she'd just given herself, she'd love to have dinner with him. And breakfast tomorrow, too. But, not only was there the whole job thing to consider, she didn't have time. "I need to finish a few things at the office and get home. I'm still not finished unpacking, and I need to get that done. I can't find anything."

"Okay, then I'll come and help you. And I'll bring dinner."

She stifled a snort, and said, "Having someone to lug boxes from the living room to the guest room would be fantastic." But she wasn't a masochist, and inviting Erik into her home would be pure torture. "I appreciate the offer, but I don't think it's a good idea."

His smile turned less wolfish and more sincere. "I'll behave. Promise." He held up three fingers. "Scout's honor."

She laughed and shook her head. "You were never a Boy Scout."

"You got me there." He dropped his hand and hunched down in front of her. "But I do promise, Erik's honor, no touching. I'll bring dinner, help you move boxes around, and whatever else you need, then leave."

Unconvinced, but tired and ready for a little company and some help getting those damned boxes out of her living room, she said, "No touching."

His wolfish smile returned. "No touching."

***

Erik stood on Kat's doorstep, carrying a pizza box and beer, wearing that stupid-ass grin again, and vaguely aware of the self-preservationist frantically waving his red flag. Erik knew this no-touching policy seemed counterintuitive to getting Kat back in the sack, but it wasn't just a ploy to spend more time with her, as the self-preservationist seemed to think. It was part of the bigger plan. If things went according to plan, by the end of night, she'd be cursing that no-touching policy and ruling in favor of full-on contact sports.

"Hi there," she said, opening the door and stepping aside so he could enter.

His gaze swept over her pink T-shirt, ass-hugging jeans, and bare feet, where a toe ring twinkled mockingly. The self-preservationist muttered, "See, dumbass, you're in over your head."

Erik gulped, finding it difficult to argue. Forcing his gaze away from her, he stepped over the threshold and scanned the mountain of boxes littering the floor. "Holy shit." Some were open, with newspaper hanging over the sides where she'd rummaged through them; others were stacked in neat piles three and four high. "We're gonna need more beer."

She laughed and shut the door behind him. "Are you sorry you insisted on helping?" Without waiting for an answer, she took the pizza box from him and led the way to the kitchen.

Hell no, he wasn't sorry. This was even better than he'd expected. With any luck, he'd be here all night, which gave him more time to make her regret that stupid rule. "Maybe," he said, laughing so she'd know he was teasing. He glanced around the kitchen, which was slightly less disastrous than the living room. "Do you have a plan of attack, or is this a free-for-all?"

She sat the pizza box on the counter, then looked around. "I think finish the kitchen first, then move to the living room?"

It was more question than statement, so he shrugged and nodded. "Sure. You're the boss."

She grabbed paper plates and napkins from the cabinet and set them on the counter next to the pizza. "In that case, I say we eat first. I'm starving."

"Yes, ma'am," he said, pulling a slice from the box. When she reached for it, he shook his head no and held it up to her mouth. "Open." She eyed him suspiciously—smart girl—but opened anyway and took a bite.

"Oh, my God. That's so good." She grabbed another bite, then closed her eyes and chewed like it was the finest food in the world. With her head tilted back, eyes closed, and pleasure rippling off her, she looked much like she had on the boat. Soaking up the sun, the wind blowing her skirt high on her thighs, her hands stroking her legs… she'd been an erotic vision if ever there was one.

He took a deep breath and set the slice on her plate before grabbing a couple of slices for himself. "Vinnie's makes a great pizza. They have killer lasagna, too. We'll get that next time."

She opened her eyes, grabbed her slice, and took another large bite. Between chews she said, "I love lasagna. It's one of my favorite foods."

He grabbed two beers and grinned. She hadn't flinched at the "next time" part of his statement; he was making progress.

She hopped onto the countertop and continued to eat while he opened the bottles. As he turned to hand her one, a drop of pizza sauce stuck to her lip caught his attention. Pizza sauce wasn't sexy. But when she flicked her tongue out to lick it from her lip, a gulp and a groan collided in his throat. A shot of adrenaline hit his system, and blood rushed to his dick.

He took a long, cooling drink from his bottle and considered his plan—which wasn't working as he'd intended. In fact, so far, the whole damned thing seemed to be backfiring.

"This is really good," Kat said, grabbing a second slice. "Thanks for bringing dinner and coming to help. It's nice to have the company."

"It's my pleasure."

"Did you grow up in Riverside?" she asked.

"Not in Riverside, but across the river and down a ways. About a mile past the plant."

Kat picked up her pizza to take a bite, paused, then set it back down. "I have to be honest. Once I let go of being pissed off…," she smiled sheepishly, "…I really loved being on the water. It's so peaceful out there. I understand why you prefer travelling by boat."

Erik's chest tightened at her soft smile and the sincerity of her words. It shouldn't have meant anything, but he was thrilled she'd enjoyed something that was such a big part of his life. "We'll go out again. Soon."

She nodded, then grabbed her pizza and took a healthy bite.

He smiled and did the same, enjoying the moment.

The self-preservationist dropped his head into his hands and wept.

General conversation ensued until Kat finished eating. She tossed her wadded-up napkin onto her plate and brushed her hands together. Since he'd finished long before her, she asked, "Ready to get busy?"

Erik grinned at all the ways he'd love to get busy, but kept the thought to himself. "Absolutely." He picked up their plates and dumped them in the trash while Kat dropped to her knees and began sifting through one of the boxes. Finished putting the leftover pizza in the fridge and wiping off the counter, he stood next to her, awaiting further instructions.

She pulled a mixer from the box and turned toward him. "What—?" The question remained unasked as she found her wide-open mouth level with his crotch.

His dick instantly recognized the advantages of the situation and rose with vigor and enthusiasm.

Her gazed fixed on his fly, watching the subtle shifts of his clothing caused by all the behind-the-scenes action taking place. She licked her lips and the impact was as powerful as if she'd physically stroked her tongue over his flesh.

Every muscle in his body tightened in response. Sweat popped out on his forehead and across the back of his neck as her gaze began a slow, leisurely stroll up his body. Her looking up at him—through dark lashes from this position on her knees—caused his cock to swell to near bursting, and its throbbing matched the whooshing in his ears.

No touching.

He clenched his fists and closed his eyes. While taking a few deep breaths, he prayed she'd find the good sense to get off the floor before she found herself flat on her back with him buried to the hilt inside her.

When he finally opened his eyes, he found her standing in front of him, her bottom lip caught between her teeth, a tinge of pink coloring her cheeks. "That was a great view," she said, smiling sweetly.

He'd given his word on the no-touching bullshit, but the little minx didn't realize how close he was to giving his fucking honor the boot. "I'd be more than happy to provide you with an even better one," he said, his voice raspy, his tone clipped and harsh.

She sighed heavily as her shoulders slumped. "That would be really nice, but I'm afraid it would be terrible... just terrible"—she batted her eyes and did her best Scarlett impression—"to have something so incredible to look at and not be able to *touch*."

Without waiting for his response, she turned and bent over, reaching for the goddamned mixer she'd left on the floor.

"Jesus Christ!" A man could only take so much. She yelped as he snatched her up around the waist and sat her on the counter. "Sit there and don't move. Don't bat your eyes. Don't lick your lips. Don't get on your knees. And for God's sake, don't bend over." He snatched the mixer off the floor. "Where the hell do you want it?"

The little she-devil clapped her hands together, threw her head back, and laughed with abandon. The act was more threatening to his emotional stability than all her sexy moves put together. Laughing like this, she was absolutely radiant. And he wanted her more than he'd ever wanted anyone.

Including Lindsey.

Over the next hour, Kat sipped her beer and did a point-and-direct, while Erik stashed everything away in the cabinets. How it went from him trying to make her regret the no-touching rule to him skating the slippery slope of becoming a liar was beyond him. But sure as shit, it happened.

Kitchen finished, they moved to the living room. Putting together a bookshelf kept his mind occupied while she unpacked books and knickknacks. He made like a pack mule and moved the remaining boxes to the guest room, then they arranged the living room furniture to take advantage of the exceptional view her upstairs apartment had of the river.

While Kat refolded and stacked the used newspaper for recycling, Erik broke down the empty boxes and carried them to the recycling container outside. When he returned, he didn't see Kat, so he followed the sounds coming from the back of her apartment.

As he approached the end of the dark hallway, she burst from her bedroom, rounding the corner at a fast clip. They collided, hard.

He threw his arms around her waist to keep her from stumbling back. In the process, every perfect curve and dip of her body molded against his. The heat of her palms pressing against his chest was like a sizzling brand, as she gasped to catch her breath.

"I'm sorry," she said. "I didn't hear you come back in. Are you all right?"

No, he wasn't even close to being all right.

Through the filtered light of the living room, he watched her eyes go from wide with surprise to a heavy-lidded forest green as he continued to hold her tight. With each labored breath, his chest brushed against her breasts. His palm rested on the small of her back, and he fought the need to pull her tighter against his jerking, straining erection.

"Fuck." What was supposed to have been a muttered curse came out sounding like a plea.

Her throat bobbed as she swallowed hard. Her body melted further into his, and the pulse in her neck fluttered wildly.

All the way to the dumpster and back he'd lectured and coached himself like a parent would an unruly teenager. *Come in, make sure she didn't need any more help, then get the hell out before something like this happened.* But right now, primal instinct was in control, overpowering his good intentions and his word, demanding he take what he wanted.

He thrust his free hand through the hair at the nape of her neck and yanked her head back, careful not to hurt her, but forceful enough to let her know she wasn't going anywhere. Surprised by his aggression, her eyes snapped wide and her mouth dropped open, giving him the access he craved. His assault on her mouth was as ferocious as a lion attacking its prey.

Rather than push him away, she accepted him fully by wrapping her arms around his neck and dragging him even closer. He backed her against the wall, wedged a knee between her thighs, and with a feral growl, deepened the kiss even further while she rode his knee.

And it still wasn't enough for either of them.

Their tongues clashed, twisting and tangling, frantic for even deeper contact. His hand snaked up her side until he reached the swell of her breasts. He used his thumb to tease her taut nipple, and she arched her back, pressing her body more firmly into his grasp.

His heartbeat pounded in his ears as his body stretched tight as a rubber band about to snap. He wanted to eat her alive, and if he didn't stop now—which was already way beyond the promised boundaries—he wouldn't stop until he'd stroked her, eaten her, and buried himself in her warm, wet body.

It was one of the hardest things he'd ever done, but as his words—no touching—thumped inside his skull, he forced himself to pull back and draw in a deep, shuddering breath.

Her eyes screamed *don't stop*. But he had to; this wasn't right. He'd given his word that he'd behave, and although he may have a reputation for being a lowlife scoundrel, he always kept his word.

Of course, when he made that promise he hadn't counted on extenuating circumstances making it impossible. But he could still walk away at this point and not feel like a total sack of shit. The look in her eyes, her response to his touch all told him that one day soon he'd strip, lick, suck, and fuck her senseless.

But it wouldn't be tonight.

"I'm sorry," he said, his voice raw and choppy. "When I made that promise, I hadn't considered the possibility of you literally falling into my arms."

Eyes wide and glassy, she ran a finger over her lips and took a few shallow breaths. "Is it always going to be like this?" Her voice was soft, desperate. "Every time we're together is it going to be a constant battle, like horny teenagers trying to keep our hands off each other?"

He scrubbed a shaky hand down his face, then proceeded to stare a hole in his shoes as he honestly considered the question. He wanted to tell her no, that it was just a phase. He wished he could give her a smooth-talking sales job that would get her into bed and stick with his plan of working her out of his system. Then, they would both move on with their lives. Separately.

The problem was, he no longer believed it would be that easy. His cat scratch fever was back with a vengeance.

"I don't know," he said, running a thumb across her red and swollen bottom lip. "All I know is that I want you with a ferociousness I have never felt before." And with that admission, he turned away and headed for the door. "Maybe I should swim home to work off some of this pent-up frustration." He stopped at the door, turned, and winked. "Sleep tight, baby."

Chapter Five

Armed with an industrial-sized bottle of pain relievers and a six-pack of caffeine, Kat stumbled out of her apartment and down the stairs to the street. The mornings were still cool enough that the three-block walk to work was a pleasant way to start the day.

Most mornings.

This morning, the walk made her head throb even more—something she hadn't thought possible—and instead of being three blocks, it felt like three miles.

Maybe if she got the same kind of enjoyment and excited rush from her job that Erik took from his it wouldn't be a struggle to get going every morning. And while she enjoyed the walk along the waterfront, watching the boats and waterfowl, it was a struggle to force herself to go to a job she wasn't passionate about.

Today's battle was amplified by last night's stupidity.

After Erik left, it would've been wise to go for a run to rid herself of the sexual energy hammering through her system. Not finishing off the beer and half a bottle of Southern Comfort while watching Erik's small boat lights disappear in the distance as he crossed the river.

Once he'd gotten out of sight, she'd turned into a big-assed chicken, afraid of going to bed for fear of lying there, achingly aroused, and desperately wishing she'd begged him to stay. She'd sat on the deck until the wee hours of the morning, drinking and… drinking some more, until exhaustion rolled in and carried her to the bed.

Last night, the plan had seemed brilliant. This morning, it seemed like one of the worst, ever.

As she labored up the Victorian's porch stairs, Rusty pulled alongside the curb, exited his car, and with his normal, clipped pace, met her at the front door. "Good morning, Kat."

"Good morning," she muttered, trying her best to make like she actually believed it.

He frowned. "No offense, but you don't look good. Are you all right?"

"No offense taken." It was difficult to argue with the truth. "I'm fine.

Thanks."

He had his hand on the front door knob, but rather than turning it, he studied her. After a moment's hesitation, he said, "I was running on the waterfront last night, and I saw Erik leaving your apartment."

Oh, God. Her heart slammed into her throat making it impossible to breathe.

"He seemed… agitated. I didn't think too much of it at the time, but now, looking at you… Is everything okay? Really?" Rusty's frown turned to a look of concern. "Erik didn't cross any lines, did he?"

Kat's eyes popped wide open as she realized what Rusty was thinking. "No! Heaven's no. Everything's fine." Sheesh, if Erik *had* crossed those lines, they'd both have been better off. And wasn't that damned ironic?

Rusty's posture was rigid, his lips pressed into a tight line, clearly unwilling to buy the "fine" routine. Rational thought fled as a million and one excuses and explanations fought to make their way from her mouth. She tried to swallow, but the moisture from her mouth had rushed north and was breaking out in a cold sweat across her upper lip and forehead. She opened and closed her mouth like a fish on a line, but suddenly, all the good excuses seemed hidden in the fog in her brain.

Rusty opened the front door, took her by the elbow, and led her through the lobby. "Let's go to your office and talk."

As soon as her office door shut behind them, words exploded from her mouth. "Everything is fine with Erik. He was a complete gentleman." Especially for breaking the kiss that was destined to end up in the horizontal shake-your-booty. "He knew I had a lot of unpacking to do, and he offered to help. I told him no, but he insisted on bringing dinner and helping move boxes…"

As the words flowed, she realized how weak and pathetic they were. She was a big girl who could have said no. And meant it. But she hadn't. She wanted Erik's company. And if she was completely honest, she wanted a hell of a lot more than their hot and spicy kiss.

She flopped into her chair and looked at Rusty, who had taken a seat and was patiently waiting for her to finish unloading. She closed her eyes and took a few deep breaths before restarting. This time with the truth. "I sort of knew Erik before I came to work here. I didn't know he lived in Riverside, and I certainly didn't know he was a client. I was shocked to see him at the open house."

At the thought of how the next part would sound, her heart rate kicked up, and she grimaced. "We met in Charlotte. At a bar. He was there on business, and I was there grieving the loss of my promotion. We… well… We spent the evening together." Rusty was a big boy; he could read between the lines and figure out that meant they'd spent the night screwing each other like wild animals. "I hadn't seen him since, not until the night of the open house." She blew out a ragged breath. "Erik is interested in pursuing… something. I told him absolutely not, that clients are off-limits, but…" She laughed. "He's not very fond of no."

Rusty broke into a broad smile. "I'm sure he's not told no often, especially by a beautiful woman." His expression became pensive as he picked a piece of lint off his black slacks.

For the first time, she looked at Rusty through the eyes of a woman, rather than an employee. With his straight, black hair falling just above his shoulders, he fit the bill of a free-spirited creative type. But his green eyes with sparkling gold flecks and a dark ring surrounding the irises were smart and sharp, those of a businessman. His looks were unusual and exotic, and she could see where women would find him attractive. Throw in his vibrant, outgoing personality, and he became irresistible.

She, however, seemed to be into guys with short, unmanageable hair with bright blue eyes that danced with mischief.

"Kat," Rusty said, holding her gaze steady, "things are more laid back here than they were at Reynolds and Ashbury. Of course, I want all the clients I can get. And I want to do the best job possible for them. I'd love to go after some large accounts and keep growing the business. But, I'm not into decorum and rigidity." He laughed. "Hell, if I didn't date client contacts, or women I met through work in some way, I'd be a lonely man."

He tilted his head to the side and grew serious. "My biggest concern with Erik is you getting hurt. He's not known for relationship stability." He shrugged. "But if shit hits the fan and I have to take over the account again, that's what I'll do. It's not a big deal. I want my employees to enjoy their jobs and create the best advertising possible for our clients. I also want them to be happy."

He stood and smiled, his teeth a white slash against his dark complexion. "I think you'd be good for Erik. It's obvious you're already giving him fits and keeping him on his toes." He laughed and turned toward the door. "Keep up the good work."

Kat sat, stunned, watching Rusty's retreating back. He'd just given her permission to date Erik. Well, "date" probably wasn't the best word to describe a potential relationship between them, but what did that mean exactly? Rusty didn't mind if she… whatever'd Erik, but could she afford the distraction?

The chirp of her cell phone interrupted her thoughts. She picked it up, checked caller ID, and saw her granddad's number. Like a sign from heaven above, there was her answer on caller ID. Regardless of Rusty's policy, she couldn't afford to be scattered, like this morning. She had to remained focused on her job, prove herself capable, and earn that VP position.

A quick rap on the doorframe and a wave of Seth's aftershave wafting over her preceded his stealthy approach into her office. He glanced back in the hallway like Super-sly Seth, making sure he hadn't been followed, then shut the door behind him. "Hey, girlfriend."

Kat figured, most mornings, Seth spent more time on his perfectly kept blond hair than she did hers. This morning, however, he looked like he'd hit it with a hand mixer. And if she wasn't mistaken, he was wearing the same clothes he'd worn yesterday. She bit her lip to keep from laughing at both his appearance and behavior and narrowed her eyes in suspicion. "What's going on?"

"I wanted to give you some information." He dropped into the chair Rusty had vacated and scrubbed both hands through his hair. Ah, so that's how he achieved the egg beater look. He yawned, then rubbed his eyes and said, "I was working late last night… Actually, I was here *all* night while you were, according to Riverside's grapevine, with Erik." He sighed and slumped further into the chair. "Paint me ten shades of green—"

"Damn." Kat dropped her head into her hands and groaned. "Is there no privacy in this town?"

"Um, no, not really." As if just looking at her for the first time today, he leaned in and squinted his eyes. "You look like shit. You definitely don't have the morning-after glow I would have expected. Don't tell me Erik's skills have been overstated."

Ignoring the part about Erik or his skills, she focused on the first half of Seth's comment. "Have you looked in a mirror this morning?"

"No, I really don't want to know. But like I said, I've worked all night. You, having spent the night with Erik… in a situation that would've hopefully included a bed… Well, I expected more from you."

Kat shook her head and took a deep breath. "Please tell me you didn't come in here just to tell me how bad I look."

Seth shook his head and tsked. "My, my, my. Aren't we grumpy? Anyway, late last night I noticed the lights on the phone blinking a lot. Like someone was making a call, hanging up, then quickly dialing again. I came downstairs to investigate and found Elise."

He looked at her expectantly, like she should prepare herself for something really, really significant. "She was making calls to various people in the Charlotte area. Your moving from a large agency, like Reynolds and Ashbury, to a smaller one, like SMG, doesn't make sense to her. She's trying to find some kind of dirt on you." His gaze narrowed and focused on Kat's. "Is there dirt on you? If there is, she didn't find it last night. But that doesn't mean she won't keep looking."

"Wow." Kat sagged back in her chair, stunned. It wasn't Elise's actions that surprised her; it was that no one had thrown Kat under the bus. She would've thought one or two phone calls would've netted Elise all the information she could have ever hoped to find. The fact that it didn't, slightly raised Kat's faith in humanity. "I'm shocked."

Seth snorted. "Why would you be surprised? Elise is a snake. You had to know she would do something like this." He picked at his fingernail and the corner of his mouth twitched. "I'm sure your seeing Erik only adds fuel to the fire."

"What? Why would Elise care that I'm seeing Erik? I mean, I'm not. But if I were, why would it matter to her?"

Seth's face and shoulders dropped. "You weren't with Erik last night?"

"Grrr… Jesus, Seth, focus would you? Erik helped me unpack after we got back from touring his plant. That's it; no big deal. Back to Elise. Why would she care if I was seeing Erik?"

"Put it this way: if arranged marriages were still customary, Elise and Erik would've been hitched at thirteen. Their mothers have been best friends since they were little, and from what I understand, they've always had the idea that Erik and Elise would make the perfect couple. Elise wouldn't mind a bit if the parents succeeded in arranging that hookup, but

Erik despises Elise." He grinned. "Any time he has to be with her, he jokes about intravenously connecting a keg just to get through it."

Kat remembered Erik's mutterings about that when his father mentioned an upcoming dinner Erik needed to attend. Picturing Erik and Elise together made the liquor-induced acid burn in Kat's stomach.

But what did it matter? She wasn't seeing Erik. And even if she was, he'd never be hers exclusively. She grabbed a bottle of Tums from her desk drawer and prayed they were faster acting than the worthless pain relievers she'd popped before leaving home.

"Back to the dirt," Seth said. "There's nothing for Elise to find? Everything's copacetic?"

Kat laughed. There was plenty for Elise to find. Fortunately, Kat had been completely honest with Rusty about the events leading up to her departure from Reynolds and Ashbury, and he was her only concern. "It's all good, Seth. But thanks for having my back. You've been a great friend, and I really appreciate it."

"Cool." He stood to leave, then stopped. "Oh, by the way, a bunch of us are going to The Office on Thursday night. Plan on coming with us."

Kat glanced around her office, then back to Seth. "I don't understand."

"The Office. It's a bar and grill where Riverside's business people hang out. After eight, it turns into a meat market, but prior to that, it's a great place to make connections. Work connections." He waggled his eyebrows. "After eight, other connections can be made if you're interested."

"Ah." Kat knew the kind of place. There had been one in Charlotte, and it had pretty much been a requirement to be seen there. "Thanks for the heads up. I'll definitely be there."

After Seth left, Kat sat her desk, seething. Frustration, sexual and professional, was becoming a living, breathing, destructive force within her. She needed an outlet, and Elise made the perfect target.

Kat stood, then looked down at her way-too-comfy feet. The tennis shoes she wore to work were great for walking, but not so impressive when it came to bitch slapping. She dug her trademark three-inch heels out of her bag, slipped them on, then stomped across the lobby to Elise's office.

Not bothering with the politesse of knocking, she stormed in and slammed the door shut behind her. Elise's head snapped up so quickly, Kat hoped she'd given herself whiplash.

Planting her palms flat on Elise's desk, Kat said, "I hear you've been asking questions, looking for something that might cause me problems."

Elise's eyes flared for a fraction of a second, then narrowed. "It's the strangest thing. For reasons I can't fathom, you're well liked. No one would tell me anything." She smiled snidely. "But that doesn't mean there isn't something there. No one as hungry and determined as you seem to be would have willingly left Reynolds and Ashbury, especially for a small agency like this."

Black spots floated in front of Kat's eyes, and the only thing keeping her balanced as her blood pressure hit an extreme spike was her palms rooted to Elise's desk. That, and her complete unwillingness to allow Elise to see just how badly she'd affected her.

Kat forced her jaw to relax and through only slightly clenched teeth said, "Rusty knows all the details surrounding my departure from R&A. There's nothing there, so stay the hell out of my business."

Without giving Elise an opportunity to respond, Kat turned on her spiky heels and stormed back across the lobby to her office, where she somehow managed to *not* slam the door shut.

She took a deep breath, then slowly released it. *Damn, that felt good.*

As she rounded the corner of her desk, the beep of her cell phone reminded her she had a voicemail from Granddad. She flopped down in her chair and listened to the message. "Hey, Katydid, it's your granddad." Like he needed to tell her that. There wasn't anyone else special enough to get away with calling her a bug. "I thought maybe I could catch ya before ya got to work this mornin'. I shoulda known ya'd already be there. I'm jus' checkin' on ya, makin' sure you're gettin' along all right. Call me."

She rolled her head back and stared at the ceiling, hoping the tears pooling in her eyes evaporated before spilling over and streaking mascara down her face. Leaving Granddad had been the hardest part of moving, and she wasn't sure she'd ever get used to him being so far away.

She closed her eyes and imagined him sitting on his porch, watchin' the world go by, as he'd say. Granddad had always worked hard, but he'd somehow found a way to balance work and time off for fun. He and Erik were a lot alike in that regard. Maybe someday she'd figure out that balance, too.

Right now, though, making her grandfather proud was her driving force, and that meant taking time off wasn't an option.

His call, and the knowledge Elise was gunning for her, were the kick in the ass she needed to get going despite feeling like hell. An idea had been forming since yesterday afternoon, and the more she thought about it, the more excited she got. She'd always found cross promotion with clients to be challenging and rewarding; throw in exposure and benefit for a non-profit and the deal got even sweeter.

She cleared her desk, found a notepad, and started jotting down the waterfall of ideas that had been flowing since leaving Erik's office. The morning rolled into afternoon and then into early evening. She was considering calling Erik, to run some of her ideas past him, when a knock sounded on her door.

Elise stood in the doorway, a plastic smile splattered across her face. "I thought I'd show you how polite society does it. We knock and then wait to be invited in."

"You'll grow old and very droopy waiting to be invited in here. What do you want?"

Completely unfazed, Elise's smile grew to sugary sweet and sickening proportions. "I'm having dinner with Erik this evening. I thought I'd see if I could help you out by passing along any paperwork or messages you might have for him."

Kat barely managed to refrain from coughing "Bullshit" into her hand. However, since Seth had given her the inside scoop, and she'd heard Erik grumbling about the dinner, she was able to keep things in perspective and see it for what it was... Elise being a bitch. Again. Rather than taking the bait and getting worked up as Elise had hoped, Kat gave a genuine smile and said, "You can give him my condolences."

Elise's brow knitted in confusion. "I beg your pardon?"

"He's having dinner with you." Kat paused, giving Elise time to catch up. "Give him my condolences."

As Elise huffed and stomped away, Kat laughed. Maybe she'd send Erik a text, just to let him know she was thinking about him.

She put her phone down.

Maybe she'd wait until later, when he was with Elise.

Chapter Six

C autiously slipping in through his parents' kitchen entrance, Erik turned the knob so the lock wouldn't click and shut the door as quietly as possible. It was a game that had started years ago when, as a child, he'd sneak into the kitchen to get extra snacks after school. In twenty-five years, he could count on one hand the number of times he'd actually gotten in unnoticed.

As luck would have it, tonight wasn't one of those nights.

Annabelle, his mother's housekeeper, turned from the stove to face him. Shaking her head and laughing, she planted her hands on her voluptuous hips and said, "Child, your mama'll have a fit you comin' in that side door instead of the front like's proper."

Erik leaned over and kissed Annie on the cheek. "Why would I care what she thinks tonight any more than I ever have?"

Annie snatched a wooden spoon from its holder on the counter and swished it in his face. "Don't you sass me."

Erik knew from experience that wooden spoon stung like fire, and he suspected, in her eyes, he'd never be too old for her to use it on him. "Yes, ma'am." He leaned over the stove, closed his eyes, and drew in a deep breath, savoring the comforting potpourri of basil, garlic, and onion that filled the steaming air. "You made my favorite, and it smells fantastic. As always."

Straightening, he walked to the extra refrigerator in the garage-sized pantry and grabbed two Budweisers. His parents were wine connoisseurs who never understood his preference to beer, but at least they were kind enough to keep his favorite brand on hand.

Annie glanced at the beers and frowned. As a strong Southern Baptist, she'd never approved of his drinking, but she also never outwardly condemned it. Except when it got out of hand. Those times, she didn't hesitate to treat him like a child and hand him his ass in a sling.

She turned back to the stove and resumed stirring the thick sauce. "I hear you got a new girl."

"Jesus Christ—" The wooden spoon spun around and shook in his face. "'Scuse me, but this town is so fuu… fuuu…" He stepped out of range of the spoon. "Friggin' unbelievable." Annie glared, prompting him to flash his special get-out-of-jail-free smile. She'd been the first to respond to that smile, and once he understood its power, he set out to perfect it. Of course, in addition to personal gain, he worked to perfect it because it always made Annie smile, and he'd do just about anything to make her happy.

Since his mother hadn't cared for the messes associated with babies and toddlers, she turned most of the child-rearing duties over to Annie. And thank God for that. Annie had been a mom who seemed to think he could do no wrong, whereas his biological mother had remained a cold, distant female who happened to occupy the same house.

Thinking what his life would've been like had his mother actually taken an interest in him sent a shudder down his spine. He'd probably be in the study right now, sipping wine, engaged in boring conversation. And worse still, he'd be with Elise.

That thought was as nauseating as it was distressing and sent him straight for the beer in his hand. When he'd finished taking a healthy swig, he said, "There's a new account executive handling my advertising. She toured the plant yesterday, and last night I took her pizza and helped her unpack." He shrugged. "That's it."

Annie kept her measuring black eyes trained on him while she stirred the sauce, which made him jumpy as hell because she knew him so well, she could probably look straight through his skull and see into his mind. And wasn't that a scary, scary thought?

He fought the urge to squirm by downing the rest of his beer, then dropped the empty bottle in the recycling container. Opening his second, he said, "Guess I better go speak to Mother."

"I want to meet her."

He whipped around to face Annie. "Excuse me?"

"You heard me, child."

"Why?"

Annie smiled and said nothing, just went back to stirring and humming.

Shit. She never cared about meeting anyone he went out with. She knew it was a waste of time. So what had she seen in him that made her want to meet Kat?

Jesus, going to see his mother suddenly sounded like a great idea. She wouldn't have a clue what was going on with him. Nor would she care. "How long am I going to have to be in there?"

Annie checked the oven and smelled the sauce. "About fifteen minutes."

"I can probably survive that." As he followed the sound of voices coming from the study, he wondered if everyone felt a sense of dread like this when attending a family birthday dinner.

He took a deep breath, then stepped through the doorway. His parents' house, decorated with dark wood, substantial antique furniture, and heavy upholstering, had always felt oppressive. But nowhere was it more evident than in the cramped study.

He engaged in brief conversation with his father and Mr. Winstead, then moved to the settee, where his mother and Mrs. Winstead sat chatting about the upcoming garden club meeting. He wrapped his arm around his mother's shoulder, which was as close to a hug as they ever got, and said, "Happy birthday, Mother."

"Thank you." She lifted her chin and studied him. "I hoped you would shave for my birthday."

Accustomed to his mother's attempts at guilt trips and manipulations, he drew a hand across his jaw and smiled—not his special smile—and said, "I did. I shave every morning." And he did; he just used a guard to keep it close, not gone, like she preferred.

After a brief exchange with Mrs. Winstead and a terse nod thrown toward Elise, who sat in a chair opposite the settee, he moved to the window. He pushed the heavy drapery aside and stared at the river, wondering, yet again, why his mother insisted on keeping such a magnificent view locked away behind huge fabric panels.

Then again, he didn't understand anything about his real mother, which was why he valued his surrogate mothers so much. Annie had loved him unconditionally and always treated him like her own. As he'd grown older, Steve's Mom, Mama Vex, had also become a major influence, especially through adolescence.

The Vex house would probably fit into his parents' home three times. And although Mama Vex had been gone a lot, working two and sometimes three jobs to make ends meet, she managed to create a bright, cheery, and welcoming home. Erik had loved every minute he spent there, and that was why he'd recruited her help in decorating his own home. He wanted it to be like the Vex house, not stifling, pretentious, and depressing as hell, like his parents' home.

Kat would hate it here, just like Lindsey would've. He swallowed hard and rubbed his chest, trying to ease the tight fist of guilt and shame that accompanied the sudden and unwelcome thought.

No matter how hard he tried to explain it, he'd never been able to make Lindsey understand why he didn't bring her home with him. Her parents were kind and welcoming to everyone, much like Mama Vex.

His? Not so much.

Would Kat understand that, or would she be hurt like Lindsey had been?

What the hell does it matter? She's not part of your life. It's just sex, remember?

"Tell me, Erik," Elise said in a tone dripping with bitterness, "how did it come to be that Rusty turned your account over to Kat?"

Not in the mood for slicing and dicing with her tonight, he continued to stare out the window. "I don't know. You need to ask Rusty."

"Oh, touchy." She settled into the chair next to the window. "Are you sure you didn't know her before she came to work at SMG?"

At that, he cranked his head around and gave her a once over. Everything about her posture, from the crossed arms to the raised chin to the swinging foot, was that of a petulant child who firmly believed she'd been wronged… and intended to make things right.

He sat on the ottoman in front of her and rested his elbows on his knees. Keeping his voice low, so only she could hear, he said, "What do you *really* want to know, Elise?"

"Why she left R&A, a large, established firm to come to a small, Podunk agency like SMG?"

Erik raised an eyebrow. "Wow, does Rusty know you think so highly of him and the agency he's worked hard to build?"

She curled her lip defiantly, but diverted her gaze. "Rusty's no fool. He knows his agency is peanuts compared to R&A." The swing of her foot picked up its pace as her irritation grew. "I've made calls to media reps and a few competing agencies in Charlotte. No one will tell me anything."

Erik smiled, even though the thought of her trying to harm Kat made him want to latch his hands around her neck. "Maybe there's nothing to tell."

She rolled her eyes. "Oh, please."

"Why does she bother you?"

Her foot stopped swinging, and a frown settled in as she studied the floor. She was quiet for so long he decided she wasn't going to answer, but then she looked up and took a deep breath. "Can we go out on the patio? Just the two of us?"

The request was made in a soft, demure tone, and her body language had shifted so drastically he found himself oddly curious about her thoughts. He stood, then offered a hand to help her up. "Sure."

The wind often blew in the late afternoon and evening, but it had been blowing at a solid fifteen to twenty knots all day and seemed to have picked up even more since his arrival. Elise's perfectly styled hair whipped in the breeze, and she wrapped her arms around her waist, shivering.

"Here," Erik said, as he shrugged out of his sports coat and wrapped it around her shoulders. He took her by the elbow and led her around the corner of the house, which provided shelter from the wind. "All right, what's going on? The whole story."

While Elise stared at the river and gathered her thoughts, Erik leaned against the stone wall of the house and took a moment to look at her. The fit of his jacket exaggerated the slump of her shoulders, her mouth turned down in a serious frown, and her brow sported a series of creases that were going to lead to wrinkles, and quickly, if she kept at it.

"My parents never expected me to go to work and actually support myself. They assumed I'd go to college, then get married and become a social wife. Like my mother. Like your mother." She turned her head slightly and looked at him from the corner of her eye. She chewed on her bottom lip, then averted her gaze back to the river. "My parents always assumed I'd marry you."

This wasn't shocking news to Erik since his mother had pushed and prodded him in that direction all his life. But he was surprised to hear Elise admit it, especially since this was the first time they'd ever talked about anything of consequence.

"Since that's the only thing they ever expected me to do, and I failed, they consider me flawed." The dejected resignation in her voice, combined with her parents' fucked-up logic, caused a small piece of him to soften toward her.

He never stopped to consider things from her perspective. Since he was three years older, he never considered her anything more than a serious pain in his ass. She followed him around everywhere he went, and he always had to share his toys with her. Nothing in this house had been sacred or off-limits to Princess Elise.

Then, as a teenager, she had an obvious crush on him that left him feeling awkward and uncomfortable any time they were together. Their parents had encouraged a relationship, and while Elise seemed game, Erik had inwardly cringed. Elise was too much like his mother. No thanks. He always knew, back in the day when he still thought of getting married, that he'd marry someone down to earth, fun-loving, and free-spirited like Mama Vex.

Like Kat.

It was ridiculous for Elise's parents to find fault with her because of his lack of interest. He brushed a strand of windblown hair from her face, and said, "Elise, that's crazy. I had no idea they made you feel that way. We've known each other all our lives, and… well, it's not you. It's me."

At his use of the ridiculous cliché, she snapped her head around and stared at him. Seeing him laugh and realizing it had been a joke, she laughed too. Pity she didn't do it more often, because she was much more attractive laughing and smiling than wearing that perpetual I-am-superior smirk.

"Would it make a difference if I talked to them?"

She shook her head and sighed. "No. And I've given up trying to prove myself to them, or trying to make them happy." She stiffened and anger flashed over her features. Apparently the lighthearted moment was over. "But I do have something to prove to myself. I understand Rusty's need to hire someone to replace Stephen. But the VP of Client Services position should have been mine." She straightened with renewed determination. "Kat is hiding something. I just have to find it."

He understood the pressures parents could put on their children. Their backgrounds were similar in that regard. They both grew up in the high-powered world of the self-important, who believed it was acceptable to do whatever was necessary to get what you wanted.

He had the benefit of outside influences, like Mama Vex and Annie, as well as Lindsey and her parents, to teach him that being born into a certain class didn't make him more entitled than anyone else. Elise hadn't had the benefit of those influences, but that didn't excuse her behavior.

Thoughts of her harming Kat caused everything he looked at to have a reddish tint. Trying to curb his temper, so hopefully he'd have a shot at getting through to her, he said, "Rusty made the decision to hire Kat and put her in that position. You need to have a conversation with Rusty about this, rather than trying to harm Kat, who's innocent."

Elise scrunched up her mouth, crossed her arms, and turned away from him. "I should have known you'd take her side."

He grabbed her arm and turned her back around to face him. Looking her directly in the eye, he said, "It's not taking sides. And believe it or not, I do understand where you're coming from. But your approach is wrong. I guarantee you, it'll end up backfiring."

Before Elise could argue, Annie appeared in the study announcing dinner. God bless her, her timing was always perfect.

They'd finished the main course and Annie was clearing dishes when Erik's cell phone beeped, indicating a new text message. When he saw Kat's number on the display, that stupid-ass grin reappeared. God help him if Annie caught him grinning like a fool and figured out who was behind it. Working hard, he forced it away and opened the text.

Did Elise give you my message?

Why would Kat send a message with Elise, rather than calling herself? He frowned and looked across the table. "Were you supposed to give me a message from Kat?"

Elise froze with her wineglass against her lips. "No."

Yeah, he was going to have to call bullshit on this one. He glanced at his mother, then to Annie. Okay, maybe not. "Are you sure?"

She set the wineglass on the table and glared at him, sending a silent message. *Drop it.*

Oh, this ought to be good. A smile pushed at his lips. "Then why did she send a text asking if you'd given me the message?"

Elise's lips puckered like she'd sucked on a boatload of lemons. "She asked me to give you her condolences."

Condolences? What the hell? "Excuse me?"

She huffed. "Since you're having dinner with me, the bitch asked me to give you her condolences."

Erik burst into laughter at the same time Elise's mother went into a rant about Elise acting like a lady. Elise rolled her eyes and drained her wineglass, while Annie leaned over his shoulder and whispered, "I like her already."

Chapter Seven

T hings were beginning to get complicated.

Erik was smart and honest enough to recognize the shift taking place within him, and that had him concerned. Despite his denial and excuses, the no-touching rule hadn't been implemented by a man intent on seducing Kat, then moving on with his life. It had been an attempt to spend more time with her. Period.

For the past ten years, his emotions had wandered, untouched, in a veritable wasteland. But since meeting Kat, he noticed signs of life here and there, and that was disconcerting as hell.

In an effort to gain control over the situation, he'd forced himself to stay on the south side of the river and away from Kat for the past two days. He still felt out of control, but business brought him to Riverside, and that made staying away from her impossible.

Which in itself was another clear indication of how much trouble he was in.

When he pushed through the door of SMG and found Luanna on the phone, he waved and motioned toward Kat's office. He probably should've waited for Luanna to announce his presence, but he wanted to see Kat in her natural environment, when she wasn't expecting company and putting on a front.

He rounded the corner, stepped into her office and... stopped dead in his tracks.

The sight and smell of a half-dozen massive flower arrangements bombarded him. It looked more like a funeral home than an ad agency, and memories and scenes from the past assaulted him at breakneck speed.

His head spun. Spots flashed before his eyes, and somewhere in the distance he heard Kat calling his name and asking if he was all right.

He closed his eyes and shook his head, literally trying to shake off the impact of the floral explosion. He opened his eyes and forced his lips to turn into a stiff, awkward smile. "I'm fine." He took a few steps toward the chair, just in case he started to go down, and glanced around the room. "Someone's popular."

Kat dismissed the flowers with a wave of her hand. "Hardly. They're all from media reps and other vendors. You know, trying to suck up and gain an edge on their competitor."

She studied him another moment, then apparently convinced he was okay enough to stand on his own, she let go of his arm and said, "Have a seat." As she moved around the edge of her desk, he snuck a peak at her feet. Shoeless, just as he expected.

"I was just getting ready to call you," she said, wriggling in her seat, probably slipping her feet back into her shoes. "What are you doing here?"

Her smile was bright and genuine and made him believe she was truly glad to see him, which worked like a giant vacuum, sucking the tension out of his neck and shoulders. It infuriated him that the memories he tried so hard to leave behind could rush back that quickly and violently.

But if he was completely honest, it wasn't just the memories that had gotten to him. Thinking Kat's admirers had sent those flowers, or at least some of them, had caused a terrible stench in the room. Something that smelled a lot like jealousy. Never in his life had he been jealous, and now that he had a good whiff of it, he decided it stunk.

Get the hell out of Dodge.

That's what he should be doing. He should cut and run before he got in any deeper. However, his feet were planted in place, his gaze was transfixed on her face, and he heard himself say, "I came to see about taking you to lunch."

Her beaming smile was like a sucker punch to the gut. He felt like a damn teenager again, asking a girl out for a first date. Terrified she'd say no. Petrified she'd say yes.

"I wish I could, but I can't." As if to make her point, she glanced around her piled-high desk. At the same time, her stomach cut loose with a grumble loud enough to hear around the block. She laughed and bit down on her lower lip.

His gaze dropped to her mouth, slick with moisture, and hunger of a different kind took root in him.

No touching.

To hell with that. There hadn't been any time constraints placed on that stupid-ass rule, and as far as he was concerned, the statute of limitations had expired. "Obviously, you haven't eaten. You said you were getting ready to call me. Let's make it a working lunch."

She laughed and crossed her arms over her chest. "I don't know about that. I've seen your idea of a business meeting. Yours and mine are not the same."

Jesus, she was such a delight and being with her made him feel a hundred pounds lighter. "Nothing funny, just lunch." Although, if he had his preference, he'd be dining on her. He'd start with her full bottom lip, then nibble a path along her jaw to her neck and then down to her breast. He cleared his throat and shot his gaze back to her face. "Have you been to Mel's Deli?"

"No. Seth talks about it all the time, but I haven't been there."

"Let's change that." He flashed the perfect smile, and after a moment's hesitation, she began grabbing file folders from the top of her desk.

As she shoved them into her bag, she paused and glanced at him. "I'm not setting foot on a boat. At least not today."

He laughed and made a mental note about that "today" exclusion. Another good sign he was in bad trouble. "Agreed. No boats. Today."

***

A few minutes later, Kat sat in Mel's Deli, questioning her sensibilities in agreeing to have lunch with Erik. A cute, petite blonde arrived, carrying two glasses of water and menus. Smiling flirtatiously at Erik, in a way that indicated she knew him well, she said, "Hey, sugar, what brings you into town this early in the day? I don't normally see you until the sun's gone down."

Erik relaxed in his chair and returned her smile with an easygoing one of his own. "Just grabbing some lunch. Candy, this is Kat." Looking at Kat, he tilted his head toward Candy. "Kat, this is Candy."

Sparing Kat a glance that lasted a millisecond, Candy said, "Nice to meet ya." She obviously didn't mean it.

Kat smiled halfheartedly, and said, "Same here." She didn't mean it either.

Erik kept his gaze locked onto Kat's, making it clear to both women where his interest lay. As heat began to build around her, Kat took a swig of her cold water and gulped it down.

Candy sighed. "Be back in a minute, Shug."

"Candy?" Kat said, resting her elbows on the table and leaning forward.

He seemed to think on it for a minute, then chuckled and shrugged. "Yeah, as far as I know that's her real name."

"Close friend of yours?" Kat grimaced and bit her tongue. Dammit. Why did she ask that? She didn't want to know.

Not really.

And she certainly didn't want Erik to think it mattered to her one way or the other.

Because it didn't.

Not really.

Erik smiled. "Candy's also a bartender, so she's friends with everyone. She works it for the big tips."

Kat paused with the water glass to her lips, afraid she'd choke if she took a drink. Why did everything with him carry a sexual connotation?

Probably because he oozed bucket-loads of sexuality from every pore, and she knew firsthand it wasn't just an act. "Uh-huh. I don't think a 'big tip' of the monetary kind is what she's after from you."

He flashed a bad-boy-to-the-bone grin, then picked up his menu.

His obvious lack of denial was like a fist to the chest. Cara and Maggie laid his reputation out before her like a red carpet—hell, deep down she knew it the night they met. But being confronted with it like this caused her lungs to refuse the oxygen being sent their way, and her chest constricted painfully.

But what did it matter? She was the one who kept insisting he remain a client and nothing more. *Put on your big girl panties and deal with it.*

Following his lead, she reached for her menu and perused her options. However, her thoughts were scattered, and after looking over the entire menu three times, she still had no idea what they offered.

Erik had the distinction of being the sexiest man she'd ever met, and the chemistry between them teetered on explosive. He haunted her dreams, and at work, she struggled to keep him out of her mind. Since Rusty had taken away her excuse for not getting involved with Erik, she began to wonder if a quick fling, just to get him out of her system once and for all, wasn't the answer.

The slut brigade stormed from the basement, cheering their cause.

Common sense screamed, *Don't be an idiot!*

"Hey." Erik's gentle tone stepped in the middle of the fray and quieted her warring thoughts. His smile was relaxed, but his eyes held an oddly serious expression. "She's not a close friend. I've known her for years, but never that way."

The relief she felt knowing Candy was nothing more than a sticky blob with an obvious attraction for Erik, much like Kat, was staggering. Simultaneously, she was mortified she'd been so transparent he'd felt the need to offer an explanation. Deciding the best course of action was to feign nonchalance and pretend she hadn't just acted like a jealous high school girlfriend, she returned her attention to the menu without comment.

When Candy returned to take their orders, Kat still didn't have a clue what she wanted, so she picked the first thing her eyes settled on, then quickly redirected the conversation.

She pulled her notes from her bag and said, "While still in Charlotte, I read an article about Mazze Builders and a huge subdivision they're planning in Myrtle Beach. It's not your average subdivision. Along with a first-rate golf course, a requirement for any Myrtle Beach property, it'll also include an air strip, clubhouse, and four-star restaurant. With all of those amenities, it's a major undertaking." She glanced up from her notes to make sure Erik was following.

He nodded. "Go on."

"They've suffered harsh criticism because the subdivision is located along the Intercoastal Waterway. They've been accused of violating some of the wetlands protections acts, but from what I've been able to find, they haven't done anything wrong. I'd say most of the criticism started with a competitor trying to squash the project."

Erik laughed around a sip of water. "That's probably a good bet."

"SMG used to handle Mazze's marketing, but they stopped all advertising several years ago. While touring your plant, I saw the acknowledgements from the Coastal Preservation Association. I started thinking about ways to cross promote." She put her hand up to cut off any potential protests. "Here's what I'm thinking. It's rough right now, but if the three of you—Monteague Boats, Mazze Builders, and the CPA— partnered, it would create a ton of exposure for all of you."

She pulled out her rough copy points for the ads and press releases and handed them to Erik.

"To take full advantage of living on the Intercoastal, the homeowners are going to want boats." She paused and smiled. "Or new boats, if they already have one. We'll feature your boats in his ads, and both of you agree to make contributions to the Coastal Preservation Association." She leaned back in her chair and gave him a moment to look over the material. "You make contributions to them anyway. It's not screaming 'look how wonderful I am.'" She paused again and laughed. "Yeah, I've talked to Rusty about this and I know exactly how you feel on this subject. But what you'll actually be doing is bringing attention to the CPA and the good work they do."

He laughed. "You're good." His gaze dropped to her mouth and his eyes grew smoky. After a brief pause, he shook his head and leaned back in his chair. "You've sold me. Have you talked to Kevin yet?"

Kat released the breath she'd been holding and got her head back onto the subject of Kevin Mazze and the project and off of the way he'd just devoured her mouth with his eyes. "Yeah, I have. He's coming to the office this afternoon. He's in agreement that they need to heavily promote this new development, and he liked the idea of working with you and the CPA. I think the plan is for me to go to Myrtle Beach with him tomorrow—"

"Oh, hell no!"

Startled by his outburst, Kat jerked back in her seat. "What?"

"Nuh-uh." Erik had such a white-knuckle grasp on his water glass, Kat feared it would shatter in his hand.

She had no idea what had caused his anger, or what his objections were, but unless Kevin Mazze was a convicted felon or rapist, she didn't appreciate Erik telling her what she could and couldn't do. "What's the problem here?"

He turned to stare out the window and muttered something about dumbass reactions, strangling Mazze, and getting a grip.

Confused by his odd behavior, and hoping he was kidding about the strangling part, Kat watched his expression alternate between angry and confused like a flashing light. He seemed as baffled by his reaction as she was, and after taking a few deep breaths, he turned his brooding gaze on her. "I don't want you to going to Myrtle Beach with Kevin."

"What?" She laughed. "Why? Is he dangerous?"

The movement of his jaw indicated a whole lot of teeth grinding, and she was clueless as to the cause. He swiped at his water glass and said, "I want you to go to the beach with me this weekend."

Good grief, rather than sitting at a table in a diner, she felt like she was in a carnival fun house, getting tossed one way and then the other by the rolling floor. "I'm having a really difficult time following you."

He sighed. "I'm sorry. It's just that… you've been working like crazy, both at work and at home. Sometimes the only way to get a break is to leave town. I know. That's why I have the Topsail Island house. There's a bunch of us going, so it won't be just the two of us. You set the rules— whatever makes you comfortable." He rolled his head around in a circle and she was pretty sure there was more teeth grinding going on… and… Did he just growl? "I think Mazze is going too. You two could stop there on your way back from Myrtle Beach."

Oh boy. Talk about dangerous waters. She'd gotten the impression from Kevin that he and Erik were friends, but she didn't realize they were that good of friends.

Could she spend the weekend in a house full of mostly strangers?

The slut brigade let out a rowdy laugh. She'd had no problem spending the night with Erik when he'd been a complete stranger. Now, he knew her more intimately than any other human being on the face of the earth.

Okay, bottom line… if she went to the beach with Erik, she wouldn't be able to keep her distance. No way would their relationship remain strictly business.

What was she thinking? She was an idiot to even consider it. Had she learned nothing from the past?

But Rusty didn't have a problem with her seeing Erik, so that wasn't really a valid excuse anymore. And spending the weekend at the beach, away from the rest of the boxes that needed unpacking and the inevitable stack of work she'd take home, sounded wonderful. Spending a night or two with Erik would be heaven.

Erik reached across the table and took her hand. He stroked his thumb across her wrist, which sent a flutter through her heart and stomach. "You want to go. I can see it on your face. Come with us and have fun."

The arrival of their meal distracted Erik and saved Kat from having to make a decision on the spot. He was right; she did want to go. It sounded like the most fun she'd had since… She couldn't remember the last time she'd taken off for the weekend and had a good time. Shoot, she couldn't remember the last time she'd had fun, period.

But to spend the whole weekend playing and not working? Did she even know how to do that?

***

Several hours later, Kat was sitting at her desk, preparing for her meeting with Kevin Mazze, when a flurry of activity at her office door snagged her attention. Luanna, the young but usually unflappable receptionist, was slumped against the doorframe, struggling to catch her breath. Her face was flushed, and her forehead glistened with a sheen of perspiration, like she'd just run five miles.

Kat was on her feet in an instant. "My God, Luanna, what's wrong?"

Luanna waved her hand to shush Kat, then tipped her finger to her lips. "Shhh… he'll hear you."

Alarmed, Kat peered out of her office, but didn't see anyone. Heart pounding, she took a tentative step through the doorway and stretched, struggling to see around the arching doorways into the lobby. It appeared empty, so she stepped back into her office and whispered, "Who'll hear me? What's going on?"

Luanna locked gazes with her and burst into a fit of giggles.

Okay, Kat was thoroughly confused. Apparently, "he" must not be dangerous, so she took a calming breath and stepped away from the doorway, giving Luanna breathing room.

Covering her mouth, Luanna tried, unsuccessfully, to contain her giggles. She seemed almost giddy, and Kat couldn't help but laugh along with her. "I have never, in my life," Luanna whispered, "met anyone as scorching hawt as that man who just walked in here." She straightened and fanned her face, trying to get a grip on her composure. "I thought Erik was hot? Whoa, boy. He said his name is Kevin Mazze and he's here to see you." She giggled again. "If you're busy, I'm sure I could find a way to keep him entertained for a while. A long while."

"Jeez, Lu," Kat said, returning to her desk to gather her things. "You scared the crap out of me. I thought there was something wrong."

"There is something wrong," Lu said, laughing as she stepped fully into Kat's office. "That man isn't here to see me, and that's just wrong."

Kat laughed and slipped her feet into her shoes. "Where is he?"

"I put him in the conference room. I didn't know how long you'd be, and I couldn't have him in the lobby. I was afraid I'd orgasm just looking at him."

"You need to find a boyfriend," Kat said as she brushed past Lu and headed for the conference room.

"I have one, but I'm afraid I'd give him up in a heartbeat for just five minutes with that man."

"Well, you've piqued my interest." As Kat rounded the corner at the end of the hallway she yelled over her shoulder, "I'll let you know what I think."

At that instant, she ran into a wall of muscle. Her head was fuzzy and breathing was difficult, but she assumed the man with his arm snaked around her waist to steady her was Kevin Mazze.

Struggling to breathe from the impact, she gasped and said, "Oh, my God. I'm sorry."

"No, I'm sorry," he said in a deep voice that vibrated through her chest.

It was déjà vu, just like that night with Erik. His arm was wrapped around her waist, her body pressed against the solid mass of his and... nothing. No sparks, no quickening of the pulse, no earth-shattering, bone-melting flashes of heat. Nothing.

Which made it nothing like that night with Erik, because all of those things had definitely accompanied that collision.

He let go of her and took a step back while giving her an appraising look. "Are you okay?"

Having mostly recovered, she smiled and stuck her hand out for a formal introduction. "I'm fine. I'm Kat Owens. It's nice to meet you."

A sly smile eased across his chiseled face as he took her hand in his. It was an odd smile, like he had a secret, and his deep chocolate eyes shimmered. "The pleasure is all mine." He released her grip, and said, "I left the map of the development in my truck. I had that on my mind and wasn't paying attention to where I was going. Sorry for the harsh meet and greet."

Kat giggled to herself, thinking about how Luanna would've handled the situation. She probably would've fainted in hopes of receiving mouth to mouth resuscitation. To him, she said, "No problem. You get the map, and

I'll wait in the conference room."

As she watched his tight, muscular buns—encased in soft, well-worn denim—disappear around the corner, she sighed. Short, dark hair. Dark, really dark, intelligent eyes. Sensual, suggestive smile. Smooth, southern drawl. Luanna hadn't exaggerated one bit. He exuded confidence and charm and a strong animal magnetism. Yep, she imagined Kevin Mazze would be a sexual powerhouse.

And yet, he hadn't prickled a single physical response from her.

Taking her seat, she had a thought. *Could Erik be jealous of Kevin?* He didn't seem like the jealous type, especially since they weren't involved. But something about her going with Kevin had set Erik off in a big way. And now that she'd gotten a good look at his friend—both coming and going— she certainly had to wonder.

As soon as Kevin returned, they dove into business. She took an instant liking to his easygoing nature and the way he joked easily and laughed often. He was knowledgeable and professional, but didn't seem to take life too seriously. He liked her ideas, was excited about the cross-promotional aspects, and they agreed a trip to Myrtle Beach to see the development should be the next step.

Still unsure about Erik's invitation, but comfortable enough with Kevin to broach the subject, she said, "I have a question that might sound odd." She paused, considering the unprofessional aspect of spending the weekend with not one, but two clients. One of those relationships would remain platonic and could actually end up being a great opportunity to further develop good rapport and maybe even get a little work done. The other relationship was destined to… get messy.

"Is this about going to Erik's?"

Surprised by his insightfulness, she jerked upright in her seat as heat spread over her face. "How did you know?"

He chuckled and his eyes twinkled with mischief. "Erik called me about it a while ago."

Her face grew even hotter, trying to imagine that conversation. "It sounds wonderful, but…"

"Erik said you were worried about the impression it would make."

It was odd to feel so at ease with Kevin after knowing him for such a short period of time, but she laughed and relaxed back into her chair.

"Yeah, maybe just a little."

"The choice is yours, obviously. But I plan to spend the weekend there anyway, so if we stop on the way back, it would save me about four hours of drive time." He added, "I don't mind bringing you back here, if that's what you want. But I promise, if you decide to stay, it'll all be 'off the record,' so to speak. What happens at Topsail, *always* stays at Topsail." He laughed and pushed back in his chair. "Actually, most of us don't remember enough about what happens to tell anyone, anyway."

Kat drew in a deep breath and chewed on her lip. "So, I'd actually be doing you a favor if I stayed." *Way to spin it, Kat.*

He laughed low and deep while gathering his papers. "More than you can imagine." As he stood to leave, he added, "I can't tell you how much fun it would be to have you there."

Chapter Eight

Leaning over her desk, lost to the world of Mazze Builders and their new development, Kat jumped when Seth bounded into her office. "Hey, girlfriend. Ready to go?"

Ready? Go? She looked up at him and blinked in confusion.

"Aren't you going to The Office with us?"

"Oh, yeah. Right." She glanced at the clock. Five-thirty? Already? Crap. "Can you give me five minutes?"

"Sure," he said, in his typical I-don't-have-a-care-in-the-world manner. "Take your time. I'll be rocking away on the front porch."

She glanced around her desk at the scattered mess. Normally, when she left for the evening, she locked everything in the filing cabinet. But she had so much to do, especially if she was considering being gone for the weekend, she really needed to come back and work a few more hours. Not wanting to make Seth wait, she organized several stacks on the corner of her desk, then locked her office door behind her.

Maggie and Cyndi, the agency's media coordinator, were waiting on the porch with Seth. "Elise went ahead," Seth said, grinning at Kat. "She wanted to get there first and scope out all the good potential clients before you had a chance to come in and swoop them away from her."

Kat laughed, but she knew he spoke the truth. She didn't like this rivalry between herself and Elise. She didn't like conflict of any kind, but she couldn't do much about it. Although Kat didn't know why, Rusty had his reasons for not giving Elise the VP position, and it wasn't Kat's place to question it. Nor was it in her best interest.

The group made idle chitchat while walking the two blocks from SMG to The Office, and Kat used the chance to decompress from the busy day. Several groups of people congregated outside the front door and on the side patio. Maggie stopped to visit with someone she knew while the rest of them filed into the upscale establishment.

A bar and high cocktail tables filled the left third of the building; the dining area occupied the rest. A brass railing ran between the two, acting as a divider. Tonight, however, both sections were filled to capacity with clusters of people standing and talking. To the right of the entrance, a staircase led to an area marked "private" where a large, rowdy crowd was enjoying a not-so-private party.

Within moments, Kat became separated from Seth and Cyndi and was on her own. She recognized a few faces from the agency's open house, but not anyone she felt compelled to stop and converse with. Which worked out well, because even though she was here to network, she'd much rather have a drink.

She'd just settled in with her SoCo and lime when the rambunctious crowd in the loft drew her attention. Sipping her drink, she watched a pitcher of beer and baskets of food get passed around the crowd. As she turned away, a familiar figure snagged her attention and drew her eye back to the crowd.

She squinted, trying for a better look, even though she didn't want to see. "Well, I'll be damned," she whispered to her shot glass. She slumped on her barstool and watched a blonde wrap her arms around Erik's neck and pull him in for a tight hug. Kat's throat knotted, catching her last sip of SoCo in its grip, as Erik reciprocated the hug and even went so far as to nuzzle his face in a nest of curls at the blonde's neck.

As she watched the scene play out, Kat's heart splintered. Hoping to relieve the ache in her chest, she tried to rationalize the situation away. She didn't want a real relationship with him anyway. Yeah, she was considering going to the beach for the weekend, but that was all about sex. Nothing more. She had no emotional ties to him.

Then why did it hurt like hell to watch him wrap his arms around someone else?

And why, now that he'd glanced down to the lower level and caught her staring at him like a brokenhearted fool, did she have the urgent need to escape as fast as her high heels would permit?

Even though his arm was still draped around the blonde's shoulder, his body shifted toward the stairs and his gaze locked on to Kat's. His message was loud and clear. *I'm coming down; stay right there.* But she couldn't talk to him right now. Not without coming across as a schizophrenic lunatic who said one thing, but constantly thought and did another.

Okay, she wouldn't just come across as one, she was a lunatic.

And she was leaving.

She found Seth standing with a group near the door. Grabbing his forearm, she rudely broke into the conversation. "I'm sorry for the interruption, but I just remembered something else I have to do." He looked confused, but she sensed Erik closing in, so she rushed on. "Thanks for the invite, maybe I can come next week."

Before Seth had time to respond, she tossed her empty glass on a side table and bolted for the door. She was halfway down the block when she heard Erik call her name. She kept walking, as if she hadn't heard. As if she didn't want to stop and have him explain it away as a simple misunderstanding. As if the suffocating squeeze in her chest didn't have her on the verge of collapsing on the sidewalk.

The tears she'd been holding back for weeks began to drip onto the front of her blouse. Dammit. Once the dam broke she wouldn't be able to stop until she'd cried herself dry. She swiped a hand across her cheek and willed the tears to stay at bay until she reached the safety of her apartment.

She trudged up the stairs to her apartment, opened the door, and slipped inside. Too emotionally exhausted to care about putting her things away neatly, she dropped her purse on the floor, kicked off her shoes, and shrugged out of her clothes, leaving a trail in the hallway as she slogged to her bedroom.

Without bothering to pull back the covers, she flopped sideways across the bed and slid the floodgates open. It was a much-needed, past-due cleansing. She grieved the loss of her job in Charlotte. She wept for the friends she'd left behind. She ached with the stabbing betrayal of knowing her best friend had been the cause of it all. She allowed the gasping sobs to carry away the fear that she'd never be good enough in her parents' eyes and the pain of endlessly trying to prove her worth. And she screamed into her pillow and beat it in frustration for the unrequited feelings she had for Erik. The stupid, ridiculous feelings that would never lead to anything but a broken heart.

As the tears slowed to a steady stream, she pulled the pillow tight to her chest, gripping it like a life preserver, and succumbed to the heavy emotional exhaustion.

The next conscious thought came as she jerked awake with a start, uncertain what had awakened her until the next round of heavy pounding broke out. Someone was trying to beat the door off its hinges and didn't seem inclined to quit. She pulled on her robe and cautiously made her way through the living room to the window overlooking the landing.

The pounding stopped, and she found Erik standing on her stoop, hands on his hips, looking around. He was probably trying to figure out where she might be since her car was parked in the lot. Suddenly, as if hearing her on the other side of the door, he turned and resumed pounding. "Kat, open the damned door. I'm not going away until we talk."

She pulled the clips from her hair and threaded her fingers through it, futilely trying to tame the wild mess. She ran a hand over face and felt the puffiness in her cheeks and around her eyes. She must look like hell, but she knew Erik meant what he said. He wouldn't go away, and she couldn't muster up enough give-a-damn to care about her looks.

What he expected to find, she didn't know, but he couldn't hide his shock when she opened the door and he got a good look at her. "Shit." Before she even blinked, he'd pushed through the doorway and bundled her in his arms.

This was exactly what she'd wanted since seeing him in the gazebo a week and a half ago. With her head resting against the solid wall of his chest and his arms wrapped tightly around her, it would be so easy to sink into him, absorb his heat and the essence of who he was, and let the rest of the world melt away.

But she took a step back, pushed beyond the embarrassment of her behavior, and looked him in the eye. His eyes glistened with emotion, and the tenderness softening his features made her stomach lurch while her breath caught in her throat.

He cupped her cheek in his palm and bent his knees so they were eye to eye. "I feel like an ass for being presumptuous, but in case I'm the reason you're upset, I want to explain. The girl you saw me hugging is Jolene, an intern. She's leaving for Fort Bliss, Texas, tomorrow to get married. Her fiancé is being deported, and they want to get married before he leaves." When she didn't answer, he looked at her imploring. "Say something."

She wanted to say, "Damn you for being so charming." But instead, she took another step back and crossed her arms over her waist. "Thanks for the explanation, but you didn't owe me one." Shrugging as if his concern meant nothing and trying to convince both of them he wasn't the reason for her meltdown, she said, "I've had a lot going on, and I finally just lost it."

***

Erik studied Kat's defeated expression as well as her makeup and tear-stained face. Seeing her in this much distress caused him to ache all the way down to his soul. He didn't understand what she meant by "a lot going on," but decided to get some answers. All of their previous visits together had been about work, or him trying to seduce her. It was time they had a good old-fashioned conversation.

He shut the door, then took her hand and led her to the sofa. Not wanting any space between them, he shook his head and pulled her to him when she made a move to sit next to him. "Sit on my lap," he said, patting his thigh. "Let me hold you."

She surprised him by curling up in his lap and acquiescing to his cradling without any argument. He pushed his fingers through her tangled hair, gently brushing it away from her face while her eyes fluttered closed and her breathing grew slow and steady.

In direct proportion to her relaxing against him, the fortress walls he'd spent years building around his heart began to crack and become alarmingly unstable. The only person he'd ever loved had been Lindsey, and he'd sworn to never let anyone that close again. But now, as he sat holding Kat, he realized he was powerless to stop the rising tide.

She shifted and tucked her head into the crook of his neck, then began stroking his chest with the palm of her hand. Her warm breath against his neck and the soft, intimate caress of her hand caused his libido to rev, his breathing to grow shallow, and his cock to stir.

He'd told her the other night he wanted her with a ferociousness he'd never before felt. And while that was still true, astonishingly enough, he wanted something else even more. He wanted her to talk to him. He wanted to get to know her and find out what had happened since the night they met in Charlotte.

"Baby, talk to me," he said, brushing his fingers along her cheek. "Tell me what happened with your job. How you ended up here. And why you're so unhappy."

Kat took a deep, shuddering breath. "You don't want to know much, do you?"

He chuckled, then sighed in defeat. All this talk would do was get him in deeper and deeper, but tonight he didn't care. "Actually," he said, "I want to know everything."

She groaned in protest and said, "I don't feel like talking," then set to work destroying that desire in him, as well. She licked, then nibbled a path along the exposed skin of his neck, sending a shiver down his spine. His muscles tensed and he was damned tempted to agree that talking could wait.

But this was important… and how bass-ackwards was this? She was doing the seducing, and he wanted to talk. "I'm really enjoying what you're doing… really enjoying it. But I want you to talk to me. Help me understand why you're so upset."

She sighed and slumped in his arms. "You're turning me down?"

He smiled and stroked her cheek. "No, baby, just postponing. Now talk."

"Fine." She huffed and scooted around, making herself more comfortable. "You know the part about the lost promotion."

He nodded. "Yeah, but start from the beginning and tell me everything."

"Fine. I worked for R&A for ten years, starting as an intern in college, and was up for the next VP opening. Simultaneously, Mark Samuelson, a client I'd been dating for about six months, had a new product ready to launch. Mark's biggest competitor beat him to it by launching a similar product a month earlier. I'd just broken off the relationship with Mark and because of the timing of that breakup and false information he received, he accused me of leaking information to his competitor."

She swiped her hands across her forehead, like she had a headache coming on. He considered telling her she didn't have to continue, but he wanted to know what happened. In addition to wanting to understand her, he also believed talking it out might help her.

"Of course, I hadn't leaked the information. And because I hadn't, he couldn't produce the necessary proof. The R&A board cleared me and allowed me to keep my job. But because the whole incident had become such a scandal, they couldn't move me into an upper management position. They felt it would make the clients nervous, and they gave the job to my best friend, Angie."

She stiffened in his arms and her face reddened. Reluctantly, he let her go as she scooted off his lap and onto the sofa beside him. She grabbed a pillow and tucked it close to her chest before continuing. "Angie started acting differently around me. At first, I chalked it up to her being busy with the additional workload. Then one night, while having dinner with my grandfather, all the pieces of what happened fell into place."

Erik wanted to continue touching her, to try to soothe her pain, but didn't want to risk her not finishing the story. He angled himself so he could drape his arm along the back of the couch and gently played with a strand of her hair.

"While Granddad and I were eating, Angie and another woman came into the restaurant. The woman looked familiar, and I spent the rest of our dinner rattling my brain, trying to figure out who she was. That night as I lay in bed, tossing and turning, it came to me."

Erik cleared his throat and put the brakes on thinking of the various ways he could have made use of her tossing and turning.

"The woman was Mark's sister-in-law. I knew right then what happened, but I wasn't willing to make unsubstantiated accusations. I didn't have the ability, or the heart, to find the proof on my own, so I hired a private investigator."

She paused and glanced at him. The tears glistening in her eyes were like powerful sledgehammers, assaulting his fortress walls.

"The investigator confirmed my suspicions and produced the proof I needed. Angie met Celia, Mark's sister-in-law, at the athletic club. Celia was lonely because of how much time her husband spent at work, so the two became fast friends.

Because her husband is not only Mark's brother, but a co-owner of the business, Celia knew about the new product launch. Angie gained her friendship and trust and then, while Celia was crying on her shoulder, Angie took notes and learned all she could about the new product."

"This Angie's a real piece of work, isn't she?"

"Yeah, she is." Kat smiled sadly. "Anyway, Angie knew things weren't great with me and Mark, and she urged me to break things off with him. I guess she wasn't as worried about my emotional health as I thought. Her only concern was timing it perfectly, so that I'd end up looking like the bad guy. She took her information to the competitor." She gave him a sardonic look. "For a nominal fee, of course. Made sure everyone knew I had knowledge of the new product and then dropped hints to Mark that I'd sold him out."

"Shit." Not the most intelligent comment, but it was the best Erik could manage in the heat of the moment. He wanted to strangle Angie and could only imagine how Kat felt.

"In the end, Angie was fired and I proved my innocence. But too much had happened. I wasn't ever going to get another chance at a promotion there. My non-compete kept me from getting another marketing job within a two hundred and fifty mile radius of Charlotte, which eliminated all of the agencies in Atlanta and most of the ones in North and South Carolina, as well as Tennessee and Virginia. Riverside isn't outside of the boundaries, but they didn't feel threatened by a small agency like SMG. I think they were relieved to see me go." She shrugged. "So here I am. Sorry you asked?"

He smiled and shook his head. "Not at all. I'm damned sorry for all that happened to you, but I'm really glad you're here." He ignored the flash in her eyes, uncertain if it was panic or interest, and sifted through the strands of hair lying across her shoulder. "Do you like working in advertising?"

"What?" She jerked in surprise, then shifted her gaze away and squirmed around a little.

"I know it's a strange thing to ask, but..." The question had been knocking at the back of his mind since they toured the plant. The way she'd been drawn to the commendations on the walls and the light in her eyes as she talked about working at the humane society and the women's shelter that night at dinner made him wonder if she wouldn't rather do something else with her life. The only time she'd shown that same spark toward her job was when she'd presented him with the idea of teaming up with Kevin to promote the Coastal Preservation Association. "Is advertising really what you want to do? Are you excited to get up in the morning and go to work?"

She pressed her lips together and stared out the window. After a long pause, she quietly said, "No. I want to do charity work."

"Then why aren't you?"

"Because I need to do this first."

She said it as if the answer made perfect sense, but he didn't understand. "You need to do what first?"

She fidgeted with the tie on her robe, causing the fabric to separate in the front and expose the swell of her breast. Which, in turn, caused his mouth to water and his cock to get back in the ball game, but he wasn't finished talking.

Jesus, when did he get to be such a choir boy?

He grabbed her hand to stop the fidgeting and prevent further exposure. Stroking her palm with his thumb, he said, "You need to stop that, because I really do want to hear what you have to say."

She slid her tongue across her lower lip as her gaze travelled from their joined hands up his torso, lingering first on his chest and then on his lips. Her eyes turned to a deep forest green as her lips parted and her breath hitched.

Shit. He swallowed hard as need pushed him to pick up where she'd left off with the licking. But deep in his gut, he knew this conversation was too important not to finish. He let go of her hand and ran his thumb across her too-damned-tempting bottom lip. No wonder he'd never put much effort into being chivalrous—it sucked. "Finish telling me what you meant by 'first.'"

"My grandfather is almost eighty, and his health has begun to fail in the past few years." Her eyes filled with pain, and she swallowed forcefully. "He's always been there for me and is my biggest supporter. I don't know how much longer I'll have him, and I have to do something worthwhile, actually accomplish something in my life, to make him proud. After that, then I can do what I want."

He frowned. "Why do you think your granddad wouldn't be proud of you for doing charity work? That's a great vocation."

"My mother and father are both corporate lawyers, and my brother is an accountant. I've always been accused of having my head in the clouds, of being a daydreamer, never being serious enough." She made a stern face. "Why can't you be more like your brother?" she said, mimicking the hurtful words she'd obviously heard more than once.

She dropped her gaze to the floor and bit her lip to stop the trembling. "They've always criticized the amount of time I spend at the animal shelter. And the women's shelter? When I'm there, my mother says I'm spending too much time with the 'downtrodden.' Like those women and children asked to be victims of abuse. They've always made it clear I should do something more worthwhile, at least in their eyes, than charity work."

Well, damn. Kat's mother sounded an awful lot, and he meant awful in the literal sense of the word, like his mother. Maybe Kat would understand his hesitation to take her home. Or maybe, just maybe, because she'd grown up with someone like his mother, he'd be comfortable taking her home, knowing she could hold her own.

"You said they said those things to you. Is that your parents, or does your grandfather feel that way too?"

"God, no! Granddad would never say anything like that." She blinked a few times, considering what she'd just said. Her eyebrows dipped low, and she caught her bottom lip between her teeth. After a long pause, she said, "He's never, ever criticized me for anything." Her voice was filled with awe and wonder, and her eyes reflected that she grasped what that truly meant... And how incongruous it was to her logic. "He's the only person who's ever loved me for just being me."

The deep creases in her forehead faded, and her eyes brightened. She straightened her shoulders with renewed purpose, and Erik's chest swelled with happiness. She ran her hand down the length of his thigh, and her expression flipped from pensive to heated. "Thank you for helping me see that."

Her eyelids relaxed as the pulse in the side of her neck fluttered, then picked up a rapid pace. Apparently, their talk was over, the no-touching rule had expired, and it was all systems go for him to slip that robe off and take her—right here, right now.

His heart rate increased to keep pace with hers as he ran a finger along the side of her neck, across her collarbone, and down between her breasts. She moaned softly and arched her back, offering herself to him, and then... yawned.

Her eyes popped wide open and she threw a hand over her mouth. "Oh, my God. How rude." She laughed... and then yawned again. "I'm so sorry. It's been an emotionally exhausting evening. When I get upset, rather than deal with things, I shut down and go to sleep."

Erik laughed and tugged on her hand. "Come over here." Gently lifting her onto his lap, he murmured, "I've got just the thing to help you unwind and put you into a deep, restful sleep."

Her eyes glittered with desire and speculation as she snuggled into him and ran her hand down his chest. "Oh yeah?"

His plans didn't exactly meet her expectations, because if he undressed her and slid into her the way he wanted, she wouldn't get any sleep. But she'd be satisfied, and he'd feel good because tonight, he didn't want to take anything. He only wanted to give.

He slipped the belt free and pushed open the folds of her robe. She was wearing soft pink panties, no bra, and her skin was as smooth and perfect as he remembered. Her rosy nipples hardened as the cool air hit them, and his mouth watered for a taste. As slowly and reverently as possible, he slid his palm over first one breast, then the other. She arched her back and cried out as he pinched and slowly rolled the taut nub between his thumb and forefinger.

The use of both hands would come in handy, but he was enjoying having her cradled in his arm too much to let go. He slid his free hand down her stomach and toward the thin satin fabric that covered his new definition of heaven. Leaning over, he took a nipple into his mouth and sucked hard, then licked gently before moving on to the other.

Christ Almighty. His eyes damn near rolled to the back of his head as he slipped his hand under the sheer fabric of her panties and his palm encountered smooth, hairless skin. "Shit," he breathed harshly. "You still wax."

Her whispered "yes" was barely audible as she arched and thrust her hips. She rolled her head to the side and pressed a kiss against the skin of his chest, exposed by his open collar, before grabbing his shirt and pulling him to her for a kiss. He captured her mouth with his as his fingers slid down her slick flesh and into her waiting core.

Her hips began a thrust and retreat rhythm, allowing him to finger-fuck her while his mouth made love to hers. She gave her body so freely to him, he felt as if he held a precious gift in his hands.

His heart hammered and his cock swelled painfully. Shit, he wanted to be inside her. But not tonight. Tonight his satisfaction would have to come from giving her pleasure.

She sucked on his tongue and he thrust his fingers harder, while using his thumb to massage her clit. In a matter of moments he felt her muscles contracting around his fingers, grabbing hold and pulling him into her even further. She arched her back and bit down on her lip, just as he'd remembered. Then, she tossed her head back and cried out his name as her orgasm rushed through her.

"That's it, baby." God Almighty, she was so fucking hot he might come just watching her get off. He continued to stroke her slowly and steadily, dragging her orgasm out as long as possible.

When the waves subsided and her breathing grew less strained, she opened her eyes and looked at him sleepily. "That was amazing."

He kissed her softly as he pulled his fingers from her drenched channel, then held her gaze while sucking her juice from his fingers. Shit, she tasted just as good as he remembered.

Her eyes flared as she watched him. "Why don't we move to the bedroom?"

"That's a great idea," he said, as he cradled her close. Walking down the hallway toward her room, he added, "But I'm not staying." When she made a sound of protest, he shook his head. "No, you need sleep. And if I stay, you won't get any." He grinned mischievously. "Sleep, that is."

He set her down, making sure her wobbly legs would support her before letting go and flipping the covers back on her bed. He slipped the robe off her shoulders, then drew in a long, ragged breath as he beat down his natural instincts and the desire to pick her up, toss her onto the bed, and follow. Instead, he picked her up, gently laid her on the cool sheets, then quickly pulled the top sheet over her, minimizing the temptation.

He brushed the hair back from her face and dropped a kiss on her forehead. Stroking the side of her face, he said, "Baby, you need a break. Will you go to the beach with me this weekend? I promise it won't have any effect on your job."

She opened her eyes partway, then slowly blinked. "Yes. But I have one stipulation."

Erik locked his jaw and prepared himself. He'd told her she could set the parameters, and he meant it. He wanted her to go, and he'd live by her rules even if it killed him.

And, depending on her stipulation, it just might.

She gave him a sleepy smile and ran her fingers along the side of his neck. "I want a whole lot more than what just happened."

He released his breath with enough force to ruffle her hair, and said,

"Oh, hell yeah. That, I can do." His smile was as predatory as a lion going after a lamb as he leaned over and kissed her long and deep. "Get a good night's sleep. You're gonna need the rest tomorrow night."

Chapter Nine

E rik sank into a pale-blue Adirondack chair and propped his feet on the top railing of the deck surrounding his Topsail Island beach home. Little Bit took notice and bounded over, then patiently watched and waited for Erik to get settled before leaping onto the chair and making himself comfortable in Erik's lap.

"You comfy?" LB nudged his head against Erik's hand. "You'd be a lot more comfy if I rubbed your head?" Erik laughed as LB's tongue flopped from the corner of his mouth, and his dark brown eyes rolled up toward Erik in pathetic plea. "You are one spoiled mutt, you know that?"

Erik absently stroked behind LB's ear and watched a commercial fishing boat get beat to shit as it struggled to cut through the large waves churning up the inlet. However, while his eyes were glued on the boat, his hearing was trained on the back of the house, listening for Mazze's truck to pull into the driveway.

Sitting here not-so-patiently waiting for Kat and Kevin to arrive was making him crazy. No, Kat being with wild-man Mazze was driving him crazy. Sitting here waiting for them to arrive was making him criminally insane.

Kevin had dark hair, dark eyes, and a dark look powerful enough to make women drop their clothing where they stood. More than once, Erik had seen Kevin raise a finger, curl it in a come-here-baby motion, and the object of his desire move to him as if in a trance. But the real kick in the ass was, beneath the dark exterior women found mysterious and ultimately irresistible, Kevin was also a nice guy.

Erik blew out a breath and took a drink of his water. Thinking about Kat falling for Kevin's charm made his stomach heave, which was ridiculous. Erik had no claims on Kat. And in reality, her spending the weekend with him was a horrible idea.

The self-preservationist may have walked off the job, but that part of his mind had been in control far too long to be completely silenced. It was like a broken record asking the same question over and over: "What are you doing?"

And no matter what answer he gave—*giving Kat a much-needed break, spending a fun weekend with Kat, following through on the goal of hot sex*—he got the same question right back again. "But what are you *doing?*"

Eventually, he faced the question for what it was. What did this weekend mean? Would Kat expect more? Would she think this meant they were involved?

Were they involved?

What did he expect from her? What did he want?

And for those tough questions, he had no answers. Besides, it was a little late to be worried about them now. He'd made the offer and she'd accepted. Now it was a matter of waiting for her to arrive, with fucking Mazze as her chauffeur.

The french door leading into the living room opened and slammed shut, startling Erik from his thoughts. He jerked around in his chair, then grabbed hold of Little Bit just in time to keep the poor little guy from landing on his ass.

"Damn, bro," Steve said, limping across the deck. "It's just me. Settle down."

Since Steve was supposed to be competing in a BMX event in San Jose, Erik had been surprised to find his motorcycle in the driveway. But once he'd caught a glimpse of Steve passed out on the couch, a cast on his wrist, and an icepack on his thigh, the answer had been obvious: Steve had taken another bad fall.

Considering he was sound asleep in the middle of the day, when it seemed he never slept, the doc must have hooked him up with heavy-duty painkillers. Which meant this was more than a slight fracture or a small bruise.

As Steve eased into the chair next to him, Erik said, "I guess there's no need to ask what you're doing here. Or *how* you're doing."

Steve chuckled, but it lacked any real humor. "I think I might be getting too old for this shit."

Erik offered a consoling smile, but didn't comment. Even though they never discussed it, the close-approaching reality of getting too old to compete in the sport Steve loved, a sport he helped bring into the popular mainstream, was something that had been weighing on him for a while. And Erik hated that he had no idea how to make the transition from BMX

King to Regular Joe any easier for his best friend.

Staring at the ocean, Steve said, "That particular vert is still twelve feet tall, but freefalling that distance seems farther than it used to. The injuries take longer to heal. The competition's getting younger and younger." He rubbed his thigh and winced. "Hell, a fourteen-year-old's in the finals this weekend."

After several moments of careful consideration, Erik finally voiced the inevitable question. "So what's next? When you're not competing anymore, what're you going to do?"

Steve sighed. "I don't know. I don't know how to be anything other than a BMX rider."

They sat in silence for several moments, then footsteps on the stairs caught Erik's attention. He'd been so focused on Steve he hadn't heard a vehicle approach. Assuming it was Kat and Kevin, he dropped his feet to the deck, stood, and tossed LB onto Steve's lap. "Oh, shit, sorry dude. Forgot about the leg."

"Why the hell are you so nervous?"

Erik, who'd been wiping his palms on his shirt, paused midstride and said, "I'm not."

"You're as jumpy as a cat in a room full of rocking chairs…" Steve's attention shifted from Erik to the stairs, and he burst out laughing. "It suddenly becomes crystal clear."

"Fuck you," Erik said, as he turned and found Kat and Kevin standing at the top of the stairs. Seeing her standing there, hair whipping around her face, skirt floating around her thighs, made his heart soar straight toward her. "Hey. You made it." *Finally.*

A gust of wind caught her skirt, blowing it high on her thighs. She laughed and grabbed hold of her skirt with one hand while holding her hair out of her eyes with the other. The movement caused enough of a shift in her body that he realized Mazze—the son of a bitch—had his hand pressed against the small of her back.

Somewhere in the part of his brain responsible for logical thinking, Erik recognized this as a payback. At least that's how Mazze saw it. But this was different than anything Erik had done in the past. This wasn't a random girl at a frat party or a chick in a bar with whom they'd all been flirting.

This was Kat.

In a split second, Erik's focus shifted from beginning a nice, relaxing weekend with Kat to dismembering Mazze. For the second time in two days, Kevin Mazze had released Erik's inner caveman, and the beast was itching for a fight. Rational thought became impossible as the roar in Erik's ears grew and his muscles contracted, prepared to strike.

Despite his banged-up body and limp, Steve (the consummate peacemaker) managed to beat Erik across the deck. Placing himself between the happy couple and Erik, he took Kat's hand and said, "Kat, I presume." He gave a gentle shake. "I'm Steve Vex. It's a pleasure to finally meet you."

Kat, who'd been staring wide-eyed at Erik, turned her gaze from Erik to the gallant knight, now hamming it up and bowing before her. Appearing shell-shocked—not surprising, given the way Erik had charged toward her—Kat glanced at Erik, then back to Steve and gave an uncertain laugh. "It's nice to meet you, too."

Steve released her hand and gingerly rose from his bow. He shook his head as he gave Kevin a quick knuckle rap and through his laughter muttered, "Asshole."

Kevin dropped his arm from Kat's back, tucked his hands into his front pockets, and rocked back on his heels. Flashing a shit-eating grin, he said, "How's it going?"

Erik leveled a no-play stare at the man, who had been one of his closest friends for years, and without any humor whatsoever said, "It's much better now that you got your fuckin' hand off her back."

Steve and Kevin laughed wholeheartedly while Kat stood statue still. Besides her hair and skirt being tossed around by the wind, her eyes were the only thing moving as they traveled back and forth between Erik and Kevin.

Shit, this so wasn't the way he'd envisioned the weekend going. He and Kevin had been tight since college, but they'd always been fiercely competitive with the ladies. Erik and Steve never competed for anything. *Probably because we learned to share at an early age,* Erik thought wryly. And, admittedly, they had shared women. But Erik and Kevin had never shared. And they sure as hell weren't going to start now.

While Erik took a couple of deep breaths, getting himself under control, Kevin said to Kat, "I'll get your bag while the Neanderthal gives you a tour." His amusement faded as he took in Steve's wrist and slanted stance. His eyes narrowed and his brows drew into a concerned frown. "Can you get down the steps?"

Steve snorted and, fronting big time, said, "It's only a few bumps and bruises. I'll be good as new by tomorrow."

As Dumb and Dumber descended the stairs, Kat bit her lip and fought off a grin. After several unsuccessful seconds, she gave up the fight. "You *are* jealous. I'd never have believed it if I hadn't seen it with my own eyes."

"Me neither," Erik said, scrubbing a hand down his face. He took her hand in his and headed toward the french doors leading into the living room.

Looking at him with a ton of pity, Kat said, "You know Kevin's just yanking your chain. Right?"

"Yeah, I know." Erik sighed and opened the door. "Which makes it even worse."

She laughed and squeezed his hand. "For the past thirty minutes he's had a huge grin on his face, like a kid on his way to the fair. I finally asked him if I'd missed something, or if he was just really glad it was Friday."

"And?" Erik asked, waiting for LB to slip in behind them so he could shut the door.

She grinned and rolled her eyes, teasing him with the knowledge of a great secret. "Something about a frat party and a hot blonde…" She turned an accusing gaze on him. "What is it with you and blondes?"

He pushed a hand through his hair as he led her through the main living area toward the kitchen. "That's a good question. I used to dig blondes. A lot." He shrugged. "But for the past year or so, they've held no appeal."

Kat seemed momentarily stunned by his admission and its implication. He understood. He was a little rocked by the words that had so freely exited his mouth, too. Hoping to save himself further embarrassment, he pointed to the kitchen off to the left and said, "There's probably not a lot of food right now, but help yourself to anything that's there. We'll go to the store later."

Leading her down the hallway to the four guest bedrooms, he said, "There's gonna be a couple of other guys here." He smiled sheepishly. "Maybe I should've mentioned that you'll be the only woman here tonight."

He probably should've told the guys there would a woman at their Friday night guys-only party, too.

After a quick peek into all the guest rooms, they returned to the living room as Kevin and Steve appeared with Kat and Kevin's bags. Both men looked perplexed, and Erik immediately understood their unasked question.

Where's Kat staying?

He'd known this would be an issue he'd have to face, not only with the guys, but with himself. But where Kat was concerned, it seemed he'd gotten pretty damned skilled at avoiding things he didn't want to think about.

He'd built the house with the intentions of freely sharing it with all of his friends; they were welcome anytime, even if he wasn't there. Because of that, he'd established the top floor as his personal, private space, and he never shared it with anyone. On the occasion he "entertained" a female in this house, they always used one of the bedrooms on the main floor. And he only spent the entire night with someone if there was no other option.

Now here he was, inviting Kat to their "men only" Friday night, having her spend not one, but two nights, and basically moving her into his private suite.

As he took Kat's bag from Kevin, he gave both men a glare that said, *You're dead if you give me any shit about this.* With a much less hostile expression and tone, he said to Kat, "I'll carry your bag upstairs to my room. Make yourself comfortable."

Catching the undercurrent flowing between the men, she took a step back from the group and said, "I think I'll go for a run on the beach, if that's okay."

"Of course it's okay." Hoping to ease her concerns, he gave her a quick kiss and said, "Make yourself at home and do whatever you want, baby."

She smiled and nodded. "Anyone want to come with me?"

Kevin smiled.

Erik glared.

Stupid, stupid, stupid. He might as well have come right out and said, "I double dog dare ya."

"I'll go," Kevin said, smiling at Kat. "It'll be good to move around after spending so much time on the road."

Refusing to let Kevin get to him again, Erik turned his back to them and continued up the stairs. He was halfway to the top when he heard Kat say, "Let me change and I'll be right down."

He set Kat's bag on his bed, then turned to find her standing, wide-eyed, in the bedroom doorway.

"Wow," she breathed, more than said, as her gaze roamed over the large suite, taking in the details: wet bar, mini fridge, fireplace, dresser with wall mirror and the king-sized bed.

The front wall, made of floor-to-ceiling windows and french doors, provided an unobstructed view of the ocean, and she headed straight for it. "What an amazing view. It's absolutely breathtaking."

He was thinking the same thing about her. Having her in his private suite seemed perfectly natural. And positively terrifying. Add in the overwhelming, urgent need to kiss the hell out of her, and he was left feeling like an oxygen deprived man with no hope of resuscitation.

The kiss in the hallway the other night had been the incendiary device. He'd thought of little else since, and waiting for her today had been like pouring lighter fluid on an open flame. He moved to stand behind her, and when she turned around, he didn't even give her time to prepare for his onslaught. He wrapped one hand around the back of her head, cupped her jaw with the other, and captured her mouth with his. The kiss was hot, rapacious, and unapologetic.

She slipped her arms around his neck and pulled him to her, taking everything he gave. His hand trailed a path down the side of her neck, across her collarbone to her breast. When his mouth followed the same path, she trembled in his arms.

Heat unlike anything he'd ever experienced shot through his entire being, and stripping her clothes off became as much a necessity as breathing.

As he slid the third button on her dress free, Mazze's voice rang out from the bottom of the steps. "Kat, you ready? You aren't being held hostage, are you?"

Erik cursed vehemently and gnashed his teeth together. "That asshole is going to wind up dead before the weekend is over."

Kat gazed at him through glassy eyes and smiled. "Well, it was my idea to go for the run. I guess I should get changed." She broke away and began rummaging through her bag. "Want to come with us?"

Erik grimaced. "Probably not a good idea in my current condition.

Besides, running's too much like work, and I don't do that while I'm here." He grabbed a beer from the mini fridge and dropped a kiss on top of her head. "I'll hang out with Steve until you get back."

***

Erik, Steve, and Little Bit silently watched Kat and Kevin disappear along the water's edge. Erik knew it wouldn't take Steve long to start with the jawing, and he wasn't disappointed. "It's the first time you've invited someone to the beach."

Erik took a drink of his beer and studied the horizon. "Yep."

"They say love'll make you do crazy things," Steve said as he watched a seagull fly and screech overhead.

"I'm not in love."

"Whatever."

"It's just a weekend," Erik contended, maybe a little too fervently.

Steve propped his feet on the railing and winced in pain. "You know it's okay if you are. Right?"

No, it's not okay. "Not gonna happen, man. Leave it alone."

Disgusted, Steve shook his head. "What the hell are you doin'? You've known her… what, a week?" He gave Erik a pointed glare. "Or so you claim, and she's already got you in knots. You're doing shit you swore you'd never do, like bringing her here and having her stay upstairs. Obviously, there's something special about her. But you're gonna fuck it up, without giving her a fair shake, just because you're scared."

"I'm not scared," Erik said, a little too fervently, once again. "Fear has nothing to do with it." A small part of him acknowledged Steve might be right, but the larger part screamed that Steve didn't have a clue what he was talking about. He didn't have firsthand experience of the pain and destruction love could cause.

Yeah, Steve and Kevin had been there for Erik and had kept him from breaking into a million pieces when Lindsey died. But Steve didn't *know* that pain. There was a difference.

After a long period of strained silence, benign conversation picked up again, and before long, they were back to being two guys having a few beers, laughing, and catching up.

After what seemed an eternity, Erik caught sight of Kat and Kevin plodding toward the house. There was a group of children riding boogie boards, and Kat stopped to talk to their parents, who were sitting watch on the beach. Kat said something to Kevin, who nodded and continued on toward the house. Then she sat on the sand and took off her shoes and socks before wading into the water with the children.

In sync, Erik and Steve leaned forward in their chairs. They propped their elbows on their knees and watched with mild curiosity as Kat and the children continued to wade out further until Kat was waist deep. The kids, laughing and giggling, demonstrated the proper technique for riding a wave. One of the children handed Kat his board and made a paddling motion with his hands. When the next wave came along, Kat jumped onto the board and took off, riding the wave all the way to the shore. When she reached the shore, she rolled off into the water, then stood and bowed to the cheering crowd.

Pleasure rippled through Erik at seeing her carefree spirit once again reveal itself, and he threw his head back with a burst of laughter.

Steve leaned back in his chair, grinning. "She's a keeper, dude. Give her a shot."

Refusing to allow Steve's comment to put a damper on his happiness, Erik stood to better see as Kat rode another wave to the shore. He didn't have any boogie boards—they weren't exactly his speed—but tomorrow he'd buy one just for Kat to have when she was here.

Chapter Ten

Kat released a longsuffering sigh and glanced around at the six grinning faces waiting for her to drink the generous portion of Crown Royal Kevin had poured for her. Crown wasn't her favorite drink, and she shuddered as the shot slid down her throat. Setting the glass on the table with more force than she'd intended, she said, "I'm done."

Erik's friends had been teaching her to play a complicated card game, one she still hadn't gotten the hang of, and the penalty shots were taking a toll. Always a fierce competitor, she'd stubbornly hung in, refusing to accept defeat. However, as the table tilted one way and the floor tilted another, she was forced to concede defeat. "Okay, gentleman, I quit. Maybe next time I'll figure this out."

"Maybe next time we'll do a better job of explaining the rules," Kevin said as he laughed and stood to give her a hug.

Realizing she'd been set up, she slugged him in the shoulder. "Punk. Now I know why Erik didn't trust me with you."

She excused herself from the table, the men thoroughly enjoying themselves at her expense, and went in search of Erik. She found him leaning against the doorjamb, arms crossed over his chest, one ankle over the other, watching the lightning from an approaching storm.

Sliding in behind him, she wrapped her arms around his waist and stood on tiptoes so she could whisper in his ear. "I need a shower."

He swiveled his head around and looked at her through hooded eyes. "Need someone to wash your back?"

His deep, suggestive tone mixed with the Crown Royal simmering in her lower belly and sent out warm, fuzzy alert signals to all her feminine hot spots. "I need someone to do a whole lot more than that."

The deep frown line that had been creasing his forehead softened, and the clenched muscles in his jaw relaxed. Without saying a word, he laced his fingers through hers and hustled them toward the stairs.

Acutely aware that all conversation had ceased, Kat turned and looked over her shoulder. Everyone but Kevin and Steve sat wide-eyed, open-mouthed, bold-faced gawking.

She tugged on Erik's hand and, in a quiet voice so as to not be overhead, asked, "Why are they staring at us?"

"Because they're a bunch of jackasses," Erik yelled, in a voice guaranteed to be heard by the group.

Laughter erupted at the bottom of the stairs, and the sounds of the party resumed.

"I don't understand why they're surprised," Kat continued. "As much as I've had to drink, they had to know you were going to get lucky."

He smiled over his shoulder as he crested the stairs, but didn't respond. Once inside the room, he kicked the door shut behind them, then tucked his hands into his front pockets. "They're shocked because I've never invited a woman up here." When she stared at him in disbelief, he shrugged and said, "This is my private space. I've never wanted to share it with anyone."

His tone was soft, his expression serious, leaving her no doubt he spoke the truth. And like that first night in the gazebo, wariness swam in his eyes instead of the normal sparkling dance.

A lump squeezed her throat and her heart faltered. "Why me?"

He studied the floor, then walked to the open doorway. "I don't know. Everything about you, from the moment I laid eyes on you in that bar in Charlotte, has been different. You made me laugh when I thought nothing could. You made a horrible day better. And you've been stuck in my gut since."

Warmth spread through her while she fought the urge to laugh. His words alone would be a compliment. The tone he used suggested he'd rather have rabies than have her stuck in his gut.

She understood the conundrum. It was confusing, and frustrating, to have someone constantly sitting on the edge of your thoughts. Especially when you thought you'd never see them again.

"I've gone out a few times since that night in Charlotte, but..." He shook his head. "Every time, I've found myself unfairly comparing the woman to you. Everything is different since I met you."

The weight of his words seemed magnified by the roar of the ocean and the rumble of echoing thunder. She moved to stand next to him in the open doorway and quietly admitted, "You're better off than me. I haven't gone out with anyone since you."

He whipped his head around and, rather than appearing pleased by the admission, he pressed his lips into a thin line and the tic in his jaw returned. "Shit, Kat." He drew in a long, ragged breath. "We're in trouble."

He might be right, but instead of agreeing with him, she tried to justify the situation and make it less scary and threatening. "It's unfinished business; that's all. You wanted more than one night. I wanted more too, but I didn't stick around to see if that was an option. Once we've had a chance to finish what we started, we'll be all right."

"Do you really believe that bullshit?"

Pfft, no. "Sure," she said, trying to make her voice light and airy and thoroughly convincing.

She stepped onto the small, private deck that held one Adirondack chair and a small table. Taking a deep breath, she pulled moist, electrified air into her lungs and watched the aggressive waves encroach upon the beach, then break against the dunes in a thundering roar. Partial moonlight peeked from behind a storm cloud and reflected off the water's surface. Lightning flashed nearby, and the sea oats swayed in the wind, all combining to create an eerie but dramatically beautiful landscape. As raindrops began to fall, she took another deep breath, then turned to head back inside.

Erik was standing in the middle of the room next to the bed. He'd stripped off his shirt, his hands were dangling at his sides, and he wore a dark and dangerous expression. "Come here."

A shiver raced down her spine as nervous anticipation sliced through her. She'd seen desire in a man's eyes before, but the fire in his transcended simple lust. And heaven help her, she was damn near desperate for everything he offered. She pulled the door shut behind her, then moved across the room toward him. The closer she got, the more she trembled and the harder her heart pounded.

His pupils were dilated, and in the dim lighting, his eyes looked like luminous sapphires. A streak of lightning flashed and reflected off the dark orbs, so full of their own burning heat. The house shook from the force of the thunderous boom, causing her to jump and cease her forward motion.

She dropped her gaze to his bare shoulders and chest, where the muscles bunched and flexed with his apparent impatience. Her eyes raked across his well-defined abs and down the thin trail of dark hair disappearing into the waistband of his pants. At the thought of tasting him, she licked her lips.

His resolve must have snapped because he closed the distance between them in one stride. He slid one hand through her hair, then wrapped it tightly around his fist, while the other slipped around her waist. His mouth crushed hers as his tongue pushed past her lips, demanding complete and unlimited access. His tongue swept the inside of her mouth with an insatiable hunger as his hand slid from her waist to her ass, then hauled her body up tightly against his.

Despite the intensity of the kiss, she wanted more. Needed more. She wrapped her arms around his neck and pulled him to her in desperation. He rewarded her by deepening the kiss and increasing the thrusting tempo of his tongue. But then, something shifted within him, and he suddenly broke away.

Breathing hard, he dropped his forehead to the crook of her neck and whispered, "God help me."

Confusion swamped her as she continued to tremble and her breathing came in short, jerky gasps. She still had her arms wrapped around his neck in a death grip, so she released him.

He slowly unraveled her hair from his fist, took a few steps back, then flopped down on the edge of the bed. His chest heaved with his labored breathing, his hands were clenched into tight fists, and the muscles in his jaw worked overtime. Letting his gaze travel from her bare feet to her eyes, he said, "Why don't you undress for me?"

It was more command than request, and her knees weakened at the domineering tone and searing look. She'd been confused by his reaction to their kiss, but seeing the intensity in his eyes, she suspected his distance had been a defensive reaction. For her part, she liked the responsive intensity. It made her feel sexy and desirable and powerful as a woman. She wanted to make this time with him memorable. She knew she'd never forget it, and she wanted to make sure he didn't either.

She relaxed her head back toward her shoulders, closed her eyes so she wouldn't be distracted by his gaze, and drifted away in a world of sensations. As she moved in slow, sinuous movements, she focused on the rain pounding against the glass, the claps of thunder rocking the house, and the flashes of lightning visible through her closed eyelids. She hadn't noticed a ceiling fan earlier, but lost in the hypersensitivity of the moment, she became aware of the faint whir of a motor and the cool breeze stroking her skin.

Continuing her languid, fluid movements, she took care of a few inconvenient details, like stripping off her frumpy, oversized T-shirt and freeing her hair from its ponytail. A sports bra and running shorts weren't the sexiest clothing, but she'd have to make the best of it.

Pretending her hands were Erik's, she touched herself in all the places and all the ways she wanted him to. She ran light, stroking caresses across her stomach and shivered as her hair swung across her back, causing a tickling sensation that mirrored that of her fingers on her stomach.

Craving a more intimate touch, she brushed her hands over her heated flesh and cupped her breasts. Her nipples were tight and achy, and the spandex of the bra was too confining. She pushed the fabric up, revealing her breasts, then pinched and rolled her nipples between her fingers and thumbs. A moan escaped her throat and mingled in the air with a hiss and muttered curse from Erik.

Emboldened by his reaction, she stroked the side of her neck, then trailed her fingers back down to her nipple while her other hand slid across her stomach, down her crotch, and stroked the inside of her thigh.

"Shit, baby." His voice was husky and strangled and wrapped around her like a caress, encouraging her to keep going.

She hooked her thumbs under the waistband of her running shorts and slowly pushed them down her thighs, then let them drop in a silky puddle at her feet. Every nerve ending had risen to the surface, and she ached for Erik's touch. Fantasizing had gotten her this far, but she needed the real thing.

She opened her eyes and was greeted by a scorching look that sent flames shooting from the tips of her toes to her head. A flush swept over her as she took a step closer and whispered, "I need you to touch me. Please."

The inferno in his eyes settled to a smoldering warmth as he reached his hand out to her. When she slipped her palm into his, he surprised her by twirling her around before pulling her onto his lap.

She closed her eyes and rested her head on his shoulder. Her bare back pressed against his warm chest, and, thanks to the nonexistent back of her thong, the rough fabric of his shorts and prominent erection stroked her ass.

He slipped his knees under hers, hooked his ankles inside of hers, and used his legs to spread her wide. She gasped as the cool currents from the ceiling fan brushed over her heated core.

Hands, rough like leather, cupped her breasts. Warm velvet breath stroked her neck and shoulder. "Open your eyes for me, sweetheart." As she struggled to force her eyelids open, he said, "Look straight ahead."

She lifted her heavy head from the comfort of his shoulder and found herself staring straight into the reflection of a wanton woman with her bra pushed up over her breasts, sitting on a man's lap, her legs spread wide. What a nefarious picture they made.

In an instant, she understood the appeal of mirrors on the ceiling. It was incredibly arousing to watch as he tugged on her tight nipples, kissed and laved the side of her neck, and nibbled his way to her earlobe.

He ran his hands down her arms and quietly said, "Wrap your hands around the outside of my thighs." She did as he said, and he tucked her fingers under his legs, effectively trapping them.

Watching her reflection in the mirror, he said, "You are so beautiful."

He pushed her hair over one shoulder and dropped gentle kisses along the side of her exposed neck, sending chills racing down her spine, while she moaned and wiggled restlessly on his lap, eager for more contact.

Grinning arrogantly, he teased, "What's the matter? A minute ago you enjoyed slow torture."

"God, Erik, you've been torturing me for days." It didn't matter if she was awake or asleep, thoughts of being with Erik had kept her in a perpetual state of arousal. Last night had been amazing, but it hadn't satisfied her as much as left her wanting more.

He moved his hand across the soft, smooth flesh of her stomach and stopped short of the edge of her panties. She lifted her hips, encouraging him to move lower, but he only smiled and dropped both hands to her knees. While his fingers took an agonizingly slow trip up her inner thighs, his tongue and mouth worked their magic on the back of her neck and shoulders.

The two of them were polar opposites. She felt the slow, steady cadence of his heartbeat against her bare back, while her heart pounded erratically. His breathing was slow and rhythmic, while she gasped for air. He seemed relaxed and in total control, while she teetered on the verge of insanity. She wiggled and writhed, trying to create the friction she needed, as well as entice him to get naked and join her in the Land of Lust.

"Relax," he murmured, as his fingers stopped their northerly route at the point where her thighs met the epicenter of her universe. His hands were so close to her sex she felt the heat radiating from them, yet he might as well have been a million miles away for all the good it did.

Frustrated, she tugged, trying to free her hands, which were held securely under his thighs, her arms pinned against her sides. His chuckle sent warm, moist breath dancing down her neck and fury rippling through her body. She growled in frustration and tugged again.

"Relax and stop fighting me. Enjoy every touch and sensation. What's the rush?"

"Rush?" she sputtered, stunned into stillness. "You call thirteen months rushing?"

He smiled and smoothed his knuckles across her chest, then gathered her breast in his palm. He flicked the nipple, causing her to arch her back and resume the wriggling.

"I'm gonna spend all night scratchin' that itch, baby. But not until you relax into me and let go."

She had never been this aroused, or frustrated, in her life. She clenched her teeth and snarled, "I want to let go, but you won't let me."

"Look at how fuckin' hot you are."

All she saw in the mirror was a wild woman in a frenzied state, desperate to get off and dangerous enough to kill if he didn't get with the program and make it happen pretty damned fast.

Finally, with whisper-soft touches, he moved his fingers across the sheer fabric at the front of her panties.

She whimpered and thrust again, and when she caught his wicked grin reflecting in the mirror, she resorted to begging. "Erik, please."

"Please what?" His fingers continued their butterfly caresses, but refused to give her what she needed.

"Please make me come."

"Don't take your eyes off that mirror."

She locked her gaze on the mirror and took a few deep breaths. The throb was agonizing, but she forced herself to relax into him.

"That's my girl," he whispered. With one arm wrapped around her waist, acting as an anchor, he used his free hand to fist the fabric triangle of her panties, turning it into a thin, narrow band. He pulled the strip of fabric up and slid it over her sensitive and throbbing clit.

That was all it took.

The orgasm that shot through her threatened to rip her apart. She tried to keep her eyes open, to see herself as Erik saw her, to watch the appreciation on his face as she came undone in his arms, but it was too intense. She arched her back and bit her lip as her entire body shuddered through wave after wave.

He held her tightly to him, never letting go, even when she was sure she'd splintered in two.

"You're incredible," he said, as she slowly opened her eyes and regained a form of consciousness.

She would have laughed, but she didn't have the strength. "I haven't done a damn thing except enjoy myself."

***

Erik swallowed hard and tried to scrub away the feelings bursting to life in his emotional wasteland. Kat may think she hadn't done anything except enjoy an orgasm, but she was wrong. Very wrong.

Something inside of him tore loose the moment he kissed her and burst wide open with her orgasm. Of all the lovers he'd had, none were as responsive and open as Kat. She gave herself over to him completely, and there was something incredibly special about that.

Scooping her up in his arms, he turned and laid her on the bed, situating her ass at the very edge. He pulled her bra over her head, slid her panties off, and knelt between her splayed thighs. He felt like a starving man on the verge of death.

As he suckled her still-sensitive clit, Kat cried out and grabbed the sides of his head. "Erik, please."

He looked at her through half-mast lids. "Please what?"

"I don't know," she said, half sobbing, half laughing.

He rubbed his cheek and chin across the sensitive flesh of her inner thigh, then smoothed the abrasion with his tongue. "You're like an ice cream cone," he said, nipping and sucking gently on her inner thigh.

Her glazed gaze caught his and her breath hitched as he nipped her thigh again. "I'm what?"

"Like an ice cream cone." His teeth closed over the tender flesh at the apex of her thigh. "A little nibble here." He swirled his tongue in a circular motion. "A lick around the edge of the cone. A suck here. Smooth and creamy and sweet to eat."

He slid his hands under her ass and lifted her off the bed, which gave him complete access to her sweet cream. He ran his tongue up the length of her slit, savoring her as if she were his own personal treat, existing simply for his indulgence. She gasped and groaned and thrust her hips as he nibbled, licked, and stroked, and in a matter of moments, she erupted again.

His heartbeat pounded in his ears like a jackhammer, and the head of his cock felt as if it would blast off if he didn't get inside her. While her orgasm subsided, he undressed and rolled on a condom, then slid his elbows under her knees, lifted her off the bed, and thrust into her in one long stroke. Shocked by how tight she was, he immediately stilled and allowed her body to adjust. "Are you okay?"

She wiggled and thrust upward. "I will be when you start moving."

He grinned. "Yes, ma'am."

Just like before, they fit together perfectly. It was as if their bodies had been made solely for the purpose of pleasuring each other. She met him thrust for thrust, and they settled into a comfortable rhythm, her body accepting his and his giving everything in return.

He slipped his arms from under her legs and planted his elbows next to her head. Dropping his mouth to hers, he lavished her with deep, passionate kisses. Rather than plundering, like before, he gently stroked the inside of her mouth and savored her tongue.

He stared into her beautiful emerald eyes that were like open windows, always giving an inside view of everything she felt. Right now, along with sexual satisfaction, they were broadcasting deep, affectionate warmth.

What about her? What did she see when she looked at him? Did she see the ugliness inside of him? Or did she see those same feelings reflected.

Terrified of getting too close and allowing that to happen, he squeezed his eyes shut and dropped his head into the crook of her neck. Suddenly, it felt like he was fighting the battle of his life.

It didn't matter that her body pulled him in, gripped him, and held on tightly. He could not, would not, fall for her. He quickened his thrusts into a relentless, hammering pace, trying to drive the unwanted feelings back. This was only sex. Nothing more. Strictly. Physical. Pleasure.

But when she wrapped her legs around his waist and her arms around his neck, pulling him in even tighter, his control crumbled. Despite his scratching and clawing for a hold, he tumbled over the edge and into the terrifying abyss.

He pulled her as close as humanly possible and gave one last searing thrust as his orgasm ripped through him. He fell into a previously unknown world—twisting, turning, completely out of control, with no way to stop and no way of knowing when he'd hit bottom. But all the while, knowing the crash, whenever, wherever, would hurt like hell.

His orgasm pulled her over the edge with him, and she threw her head back, cried out his name on a sob, and arched her body into his.

Too exhausted to move, he rested his head in the safety of the crook of her neck and held her tight as their breathing and hearts settled. When she released her grip on his neck, he lifted his head and risked glancing into her eyes.

And had his heart ripped from his chest.

"Kat?" he whispered, running a thumb over her damp cheek. "Why are you crying?"

She took a deep, shuddering breath and gave him a quivering smile. "I don't know what happened. All I know is that it was so intense I started to cry, and I couldn't hold back the tears. I've never had that happen before." Looking embarrassed, and trying to lighten the moment, she giggled and said, "What did you do to me?"

More than happy to go along with the humor, he waggled his brow and said, "Old Erik secret." Feeling as if his legs were strong enough to carry him to the bathroom, he kissed her on top of the head, and prepared to make his escape. "I'll be right back."

As he struggled to maintain his cool on the trek to the head, her words echoed through his mind. *What did you do to me?*

He should be the one asking her that, because he knew, without a shadow of a doubt, he was not the same man he'd been an hour ago.

Chapter Eleven

With achy muscles moaning in protest, reminding her of the delicious workout they received the night before, Kat eased into the Adirondack chair on the large deck surrounding Erik's house. The morning air was cool, but the brilliant sunshine quickly warmed her skin. She propped her bare feet on the railing, then relaxed into the chair with a bagel and a bottle of water.

The sun's morning rays reflecting off the slow-crawling ocean waves created a magnificent picture. But the sight of Erik playing ball on the beach with Little Bit was breathtaking. He wore only loose-fitting swimming trunks that hung low on his waist. The muscles in his arms, back, and shoulders bunched and flexed in a spectacular display as he leaned back and launched the ball into a high arc.

Her fingers twitched with the memory of how those lean muscles had felt under her fingertips as he'd arched away, then plunged back into her. Waking, wrapped in the cocoon of his embrace, would have been the perfect way to start the day. But it hadn't surprised her to wake alone.

Throughout the night, she'd felt like she was making love… no, no, no… having sex with a rubber band. At times, they were so close emotionally it was like their souls were fusing into one. And then, when things got too intense, Erik would snap back, emotionally recoiling.

Their wild and reckless adventure in Charlotte had been all about trying to make a bad day better. It had been nothing more than a detached comforting, and exquisite physical release. There had been spinning and flipping and feats of contortionism that had made them laugh as they'd entwined like twist ties. There had been little full-frontal contact and minimal prolonged eye contact.

But last night, emotions had come into play. On both sides. Whether he admitted it or not, Erik cared for her. She knew that wasn't part of his plan. Hell, it hadn't been part of her plan, either. But the tenderness etched on his face as he held tight and drove deeply into her couldn't be denied.

Little Bit's whining and scratching at the door this morning had given him the perfect excuse to leave the room and have some space. She hadn't seen the point in getting up and rushing things; they'd have to face the consequences of the night soon enough. So, while he spaced it somewhere else, she took advantage of the quiet and got some much needed sleep.

However, she couldn't put off the inevitable any longer. It was time to see how much damage had been inflicted and make sure there weren't going to be any residual problems with their working relationship.

She brushed the bagel's crumbs from her tank top, took a drink of water to wash down the clump stuck in her throat, then meandered down to the beach. She waited while Erik threw the ball, then said, "Good morning."

His smile was large and genuine as he turned and gave her a quick kiss. "Mornin'. How'd ya sleep?"

His easy, suggestive drawl tempted her to believe her concerns about the potential fallout were unfounded, and she began to relax. "What little I got was great."

He smiled like an arrogant male who knew just how completely he'd satisfied his partner, and he was damned proud of it. But then, as if realizing they were getting too cozy, his demeanor shifted, and he went into retreat and withdrawal mode again.

Sheesh, and men claim women are moody?

Little Bit returned with the ball, and Erik busied himself by wrestling it away, then throwing it again.

Irritated, mostly that she'd been foolish enough to think this could work without serious repercussions, she blew out a breath and said, "Look, Erik…"

He turned to her, and the rest of the words hit a roadblock in her throat. Instead of the usual sparkling irises, his eyes were dull, flat orbs.

She hated the strain on his face, and a throb of regret pulsed through her. "My coming here was obviously a bad idea. When Kevin gets back from fishing, I'll ask him if he minds taking me back to Riverside. Or… maybe Seth would come and pick me up."

His eyebrows drew into a harsh line over narrowed eyes. "Are you always like this?"

She took a step back, startled by his harsh snap. "Excuse me?"

"Do I ever get a say in what happens between us?" He slammed his hands onto his hips, sending the loose-fitting trunks lower on his waist, and a chill flushed through her at his glower. "It's like Charlotte all over again. Suddenly, you've decided it's a bad idea and you're gonna run off again. I thought things were pretty damned good."

A cool wave rushed around her ankles, anchoring her feet in the cold, wet sand as anger washed through her. The heaviness of the sand matched the weight in her chest as she struggled to breathe. "Yeah, last night things were great." She challenged him with an angry look of her own. "But this morning, there's more than a little regret floating around in the air, and you obviously need more space." She took a calming breath and said, "I just want to make sure things don't get any more awkward and that we're able to persevere a decent working relationship."

He exhaled like she'd punched him in the stomach, then stepped forward and wrapped her in a hug that threatened to squeeze the life out of her. "I don't need space, Kat, and I'm sorry I made you feel that way." He propped his chin on top of her head and sighed. "I… shit… I don't know what to do with you."

His flip-flopping mood kept her confused and guarded, but she couldn't resist resting her head on his chest and returning the hug. Sliding her fingers along the ridge of his spine, she muttered, "You seemed to know exactly what to do with me last night."

"Smartass." He kept his arms wrapped around her waist, but drew back so he could look at her. "I looked up there and saw you sitting on the deck, and it was just like last night when you were walking around my bedroom. It seemed perfectly natural, like you belonged there." He stroked the backs of his knuckles across her cheek. "My usual tactics of making sure I don't get too close aren't working with you." He laughed. "Hell, I guess that's no surprise, since I'm not even trying to stick to my normal tactics."

Kat wiggled her toes in the wet sand and verbally tippy toed into his personal history. "Why do you try so hard to avoid relationships?" Realizing how the question might sound, she said, "I'm not pushing for one; I'm just curious. Normally, when someone works that hard to avoid something, they have a very strong reason."

He released her and took the ball from Little Bit, then tossed it down the beach before settling his gaze on the horizon. "I had a fiancée once. Well, an almost-fiancée."

The agony in his voice and the haunted memories in his eyes sent a sharp pang through her chest. She wanted to reach out to him, but he seemed lost in time, and she didn't want to interrupt his thoughts.

"I swore I'd never get that close to anyone again." He grimaced, although she thought he was trying to smile. "I did all right until you came along. But after last night, I want you now more than ever, and I don't know how to handle that."

She didn't know what to say. His past was still so obviously painful she wished she could help extinguish the hurt, but she didn't know how. She'd also never received a declaration of affection quite so half-assed, and even though it wasn't meant to be, it was a declaration. And probably as much of one as she'd ever get from Erik.

Sensing another impending withdrawal, she decided to leave first and give him space before he could emotionally pull away again. "I think I'll go for a run." Running was her way of working through life's difficulties, and right now, it seemed like the perfect solution.

He took her hand in his and caressed her wrist. "I don't want you to go. I mean, going for a run is fine. But I don't want you to go back to Riverside. Needing you like I do terrifies me, but the thought of not seeing you makes me crazy." He watched the wave breaking around his ankles, seemingly noticing for the first time he stood in the water. His mouth twisted into a wry smile and he said, "I think I'm in too deep."

She didn't know if he meant the water or with her, but she suspected both. "I'll stay for a little while. Let's see how things go throughout the day and we'll reevaluate. Okay?"

He smiled and tugged her closer for a kiss. "Deal."

As she made her way back to the house, she considered everything Erik had said. She understood his perspective. She spent thirteen months thinking about him. She hadn't dated anyone else because no one else could compare, and she began to think he ruined her. Yet, she was foolish enough to think they could have a couple of hot nights, finish the business they started in Charlotte and then move on with their separate lives.

Maybe last night when he said, "We're in trouble," she should've heeded his warning. But she couldn't have stopped last night from happening any more than she could stop the incoming tide. The desire between them, the sparks, the connection—it was all too powerful, and she was defenseless against its enormity.

But what did they do now? If anything, the connection had grown stronger, and she was incapable of severing it.

The beeping of her cell phone disrupted her runaway thoughts as she rummaged through her bag, looking for a sports bra and running shorts. She knew, without looking, it was another missed call from Granddad.

Carrying the phone to the deck, she felt like a piece of driftwood that had been tossed around by the pounding surf, then left behind on the sandy beach. A grounding conversation with him was exactly what she needed.

After two rings she heard, "How's my Katydid?"

The familiarity of his voice soothed her soul. She smiled, thinking back to the day she'd gotten him the new phone with caller ID. The idea of knowing who was calling before he answered had intrigued him, and he'd obviously gotten the hang of using it. "Hi, Granddad. I'm fine."

"Ya don't sound fine." Concern laced his words.

Instead of sitting in the chair, she sat on the deck and rested her forehead against the spindles of the deck railing. She drew in a ragged breath and considered lying. But he knew her too well to be deceived, so she opted for the truth. "I'm an idiot."

His chuckle warmed her heart and made her feel like a little girl again. She futilely wished she could crawl into his lap, let him brush his hand over her hair, and reassure her everything would be okay.

"I'll never believe that. What's goin' on?"

Kat glanced out at the beach where Erik sat with his elbows resting on bent knees, his head dropped into his hands. He looked as miserable as she felt. "You're never going to believe I could be this stupid, but..." She squeezed her eyes shut and swallowed hard as the depth of her feelings for Erik overwhelmed her. "Oh God, I think I've fallen in love." She paused. "With a client."

"What's the matter with that?"

She groaned. "I thought I was smarter than this."

"There's nothin' wrong with fallin' in love. It's the best thing that can ever happen to ya. As long as it's the right guy."

"That's the problem; he's a client, which makes him the wrong guy."

He also doesn't want to love me back. She didn't believe for a second Erik didn't care, but he was so conflicted over his feelings, he'd fight them to the end.

"Katy, why do you keep doin' this?"

She laughed to keep from crying. "Because I'm an idiot. I just said that."

"I mean, why do ya keep puttin' a job… a job ya don' even like… above ever'thing else?" She didn't have a chance to answer before he started again. "Are ya volunteerin' at the animal shelter? Have ya found the women's shelter and gone over there 'n done some work?"

"No, sir."

"Why not?"

"Because I don't have time. I'm trying to be responsible and give all of my time and effort to my new job. Those other things are what you do in your spare time, and I don't have any of that right now."

"Horse malarkey. You listen to me. Your mama is my only child, and I love her. But she's full of crap. I shoulda said this long ago, but I've tried to mind my own business. You've let that high fallutin' mother of yours fill your head with a bunch of garbage. Life is about more than makin' a pile of money. As long as ya got enough to eat and have a roof over your head, it don' matter about nothin' else. Volunteerin's important to ya, it makes ya happy." His voice softened. "Are ya happy?"

Kat swiped away a tear with the back of her hand. "No, not really. I haven't been happy in a long time."

"There's more important things in life than work, Katydid. Things like love and family." His voice grew so soft she could barely hear him. "Your grandma taught me that. And she was right."

"I don't know anything about love."

"Sure ya do. Yer heart's overflowin' with it. That's why ya do the things ya do. Goin' to the homeless shelter on Christmas mornin' to feed the folks there. Spendin' your spare time and extra money on the kids at the women's shelter. Stayin' up all night with a howlin' cat that's havin' kittens. That's who ya are. And bein' a good person is more important than any job you'll ever do. Don't ya forget it."

Kat swiped at the now free-flowing tears and laughed, remembering the night the Siamese cat at the shelter had gone into labor. She'd taken the mother-to-be home and ended up calling her granddad in the middle of the night for help. The cat had howled so badly and made such terrible noises, they had to trade off taking care of her so they didn't lose their minds.

Not wanting her granddad to be worried and think she never had any fun, she said, "I'm actually at the beach right now with Erik. The client."

She told him about the Mazze building project and how they planned to promote the new development and incorporate donations to the CPA. She told him about learning to boogie board and the unsuccessful attempt by Erik's friends to teach her to play their card game.

By the time she disconnected, they'd been on the phone for thirty minutes. She still had a lot to figure out, but she felt like the weight of the world had been lifted from her chest and shoulders. She missed her granddad, and since the only family he had left in Charlotte was her mother, Kat wondered if she could convince him to move to the coast with her.

***

The second Kat left for her run, Erik drove to the local surf shop and bought Kat her very own boogie board. Whether she would actually use it or not, he didn't know. But the kids next door were already in the water, and he wanted her to have it. What she did with it was up to her.

After returning to the house, he wandered around a bit feeling lost, even though he was in his own space. It wasn't noon yet, but he was at the beach and needed a drink, so he cracked open a beer and parked himself in one of the deck chairs. The tightly-coiled spring wrapped around his gut had just started to relax when Steve and Kevin came back from their unsuccessful fishing trip.

"What's going on?" Steve asked, shoving his sunglasses up on his head.

Erik shrugged. "Nothing. Kat's gone for a run, and I'm hanging out."

"Yeah, I see that." Steve crossed his arms over his chest. "And drinking at eleven in the morning. You haven't done that in years."

Steve's tough guy act would have been way more impressive without the listing pose and bulky cast, and, although he tried, Erik couldn't hold back his laugh.

"She's getting to you."

That put the lockdown on Erik's laughter. "Have you always been this nosey, and I just never noticed?"

"Yeah, pretty much."

Kevin, who'd been watching the surf and pretending not to listen, piped in. "Don't blow this."

"There's nothing to blow. Christ!" Erik's irritation escalated as the need to defend himself grew. "It was one night." *Liar.* "Okay, after tonight it'll have been two. Mind your own damn business."

"I like her. I don't want her hurt." Although Kevin's words were non-threatening and his tone remained steady, his stance and demeanor were challenging. "If you're not that interested, it certainly wouldn't be a hardship for me to carry her sweet little ass back to Riverside—"

The rest of Kevin's sentence was engulfed by Erik's all-consuming rage. He was out of his chair with Kevin slammed against the exterior wall of the house before any of them could blink. "Stay the hell away from her. If I see you touch her again, I'll break your fucking arm. Are we clear?"

Kevin stood a few inches shorter than Erik, but had at least twenty pounds of muscle to his advantage. However, instead of fighting back, the bastard smiled.

Erik's reaction had confirmed Steve's comment. Kat was getting to him.

Kevin's gaze locked with Erik's like two bulls locking horns, and his expression said it all. He wasn't interested in Kat, but he would use their competitiveness to force Erik into owning his feelings for her. "Don't be an idiot, Erik. What happened to Lindsey wasn't your fault. But if you lose Kat, you'll only have yourself to blame."

Erik gave Kevin a shove, then let go of his shirt and turned away. Leave it to these two assholes, the two guys who were supposed to be his closest friends, to break out the knives and slice him open.

Shit, he needed to go make a few enemies. Maybe they'd be less vicious than his supposed friends.

Chapter Twelve

K at leaned in close to the mirror and gently... very, very gently... swiped a generous portion of moisturizer over her sunburned cheeks, nose, and forehead. The bass from the music downstairs reverberated off the bathroom walls, and the noise from the crowd grew louder with each passing moment.

Erik had warned her that, while Friday nights were reserved as the guys' night to howl and included only his closest friends, Saturday nights were a free-for-all. And from the sounds leaching through the floor, he hadn't exaggerated.

She straightened and studied her reflection. A splash of foundation would be helpful, but the thought of touching her skin again, with anything other than aloe vera, made her cringe. She shook her head and muttered, "How could you possibly have forgotten sunscreen?"

After talking with her granddad, running as far and fast as possible had been the only thing on her mind. When she returned, Steve met her on the beach with a bottle of water and a clear you-don't-want-to-go-up-there expression on his face. She didn't know what happened, but the body language between Erik and Kevin had been tense all day. And though she didn't have any way to confirm it, she suspected it had something to do with her.

Erik showed up a few minutes behind Steve, carrying a hot-pink boogie board. They spent the rest of the afternoon on the beach, swimming, playing volleyball, and just hanging out. Although tension was running high between Kevin and Erik, things with her and Erik had been great, so she agreed to stay another night.

She knew their issues hadn't miraculously solved themselves, and she worried how things would be once they went back to Riverside. But she enjoyed herself tremendously throughout the day and planned to do the same this evening. Real life would intrude soon enough.

She slipped into a simple sundress, pulled her hair up into a loose knot, stepped into sandals, then headed downstairs. As she neared the bottom of the steps, she used the height advantage of the stairs to see over the large crowd and scanned the room, searching for Erik… And found him.

"I'll be damned," she muttered, while crossing her arms over her chest. "At least this one's not blonde."

***

Large crowd. Thumping music. Flowing drinks. A typical Saturday night, and Erik was in his element.

So why did it feel like a noose was tied around his neck and no matter how deep a breath he took, he couldn't get enough air? Normally, he fed off the vibrating energy of the crowd. But not tonight. Tonight, he'd rather be in a quiet place with Kat, alone.

As he searched the crowd for her, the fine hairs on the back of his neck prickled with unease and a puddle of dread settled in the pit of his stomach. A heavy, spicy fragrance settled around him, and he closed his eyes while muttering a curse. He didn't need to turn around to know Lizbeth was closing in on him from behind. The scent was as bold and memorable as the woman who wore it. Brassy and audacious, her presence could be felt before she was visible.

He hadn't seen her in two years and didn't know she was back in town. Town being Riverside. He couldn't imagine how she knew about this house, or who had invited her. But then again, Lizbeth knew everything and did whatever she wanted. And she sure didn't need an invitation to show up at a party.

Warm breath licked the back of his neck. "Hey, sugar." The husky purr proved his intuition correct. "You look good enough to eat."

Two years ago… hell, fourteen months ago… those words from her mouth would have been the starting gun to a night of nonstop sex. Now, he had no desire to mix and mingle anything with Lizbeth.

He turned his head slightly while shifting his body out of striking distance. His best bet was to cut this short and find Kat as soon as possible. The last thing he wanted was another misunderstanding like the one at The Office. "Hey, Lizbeth, good to see you." He glanced around, making it obvious he was looking for someone. "If you'll excuse me—"

Her arm snaked around his waist, preventing his escape. "Where are you off to in such a hurry?"

While he continued to search for Kat, Lizbeth sidled closer and wrapped her body around his. She was tall and slender, and at one time, he'd considered the fit of her body against his to be a good thing. She wrapped her long fingers around his neck, leaned in, and nibbled at his earlobe.

At that instant his gaze landed on Kat, standing on the stairs, seemingly stunned and frozen in place. His breath stalled while his heart took a flying leap, as if trying to reach her on its own. He knew his eyes were screaming, "This isn't what it looks like." But Kat either didn't get the message or didn't believe it. Disappointment flashed in her eyes, then she let her arms fall to her side and moved off the steps and out of sight.

"Shit, Lizbeth. Stop." He pulled his head away and unwrapped her fingers from his neck.

She leaned back and formed those full, glossy lips into a frowny pout. "You're normally much happier to see me."

He turned to face her fully, making sure she knew he was serious and not just playing hard to get. "That was before."

It took her almost a full minute before she let go of his hand and stepped back. "You're serious." Her eyes were large and reflected an uncharacteristic vulnerability as she searched his face for answers. "Before what?"

Before Kat. Hell, everything in his life seemed to be relegated to one of two segments: Before Kat. After Kat.

He didn't want to say, "I've met someone," because that implied he was in a relationship. However, having no interest in Lizbeth had everything to do with Kat. If it weren't for her, he'd have Lizbeth in one of the guest rooms, half undressed. Actually, he probably wouldn't bother undressing her. He'd just slide her obscenely short skirt up two inches, lay her over the dresser, and go at it.

Now, the thought made him nauseous.

Rather than trying to explain any of it, he shook his head and said, "Sorry. I've gotta go."

He considered pointing her in Kevin's direction, but decided to leave well enough alone. Anxious to find Kat, he left a stunned and bewildered Lizbeth standing there alone.

***

Kat found Steve on the deck, leaning against the deck railing, nursing a bottle of Southern Comfort. She stepped up next to him, took the bottle from his hand, and helped herself to a generous swig. She took a moment to enjoy the comforting heat flowing down her throat, then licked the residue from her lips and smiled. "Thanks. Sorry to help myself, but it was an emergency."

Steve laughed, then shifted his gaze beyond her, just as her body started to hum like a tuning fork—an infallible indication Erik was nearby.

His hand pressed tentatively against the small of her back, and his voice was unsteady as he murmured, "Hey," in her ear.

A smile tugged at the corners of her mouth as she registered the hesitancy of his touch and recalled the panic she'd seen in his eyes. Seeing the redhead wrapped around him had hurt, but only because it reminded her of whom and what he was. It had been enough to send her in search of fresh air and liquid solace. But she recognized the come-on as being one-sided, and realized Erik wasn't interested in the redhead's offerings. At least not tonight.

She turned into him and held up Steve's bottle. "Want a swig?"

Obviously relieved she hadn't smacked him in the side of the head with the bottle, his shoulders sagged and he exhaled sharply. "No thanks. I'll grab a beer."

After grabbing a beer from the cooler, he wrapped his arm around her shoulder and gave Steve a *get lost* look. "I need to talk to Kat."

Steve nodded and shifted his weight to the other foot. "Okay."

Erik's eyes narrowed to dangerous slits as irritation rippled off him.

Even though she hadn't offered an explanation for swooping in and stealing his bottle, Steve had to have suspected Erik of doing something to upset her. Erik's nervous behavior confirmed Steve's suspicions, and she appreciated his concern for her.

She laughed and gave him a hug. "It's okay, Steve. I promise I won't hurt him."

Steve chucked her on the chin. "I could care less about him." He shot Erik a warning look, then took his bottle and ambled off toward the french doors.

Erik opened his mouth to speak, but she cut him off. "You don't owe me any explanations. I've heard all about your lifestyle. I know you don't do relationships. I know you don't date women more than a couple of times. I understand this"—she motioned between them—"is only for a weekend."

"Christ. There you go again," Erik yelled, throwing his hand in the air in frustration. "Making decisions for me."

She'd never heard Erik upset before and, based on the shocked expressions of those standing nearby, it wasn't a common occurrence.

She opened and closed her mouth a couple of times, but kept coming up empty. She did keep making those decisions, but out of self-preservation and fear that if she didn't constantly remind herself what to expect, she'd end up crushed.

He grabbed her hand and dragged her across the deck, down the stairs, and out onto the beach. "I'm sorry for yelling." He ran a hand through his hair, something she noticed him doing a lot when agitated, and said, "Will you walk with me?"

As they headed down the beach, away from the house and crowd, Kat asked, "Who is she?"

"Lizbeth Sampson. I... dated her a few years ago."

Kat smiled at his attempted diplomacy. She didn't believe for a second he'd dated that woman. Screwed her senseless, no doubt, but not dated.

"She moved away, and I didn't know she was back. I don't even know how she knew about this house because I haven't seen her since I built it." He attempted a laugh. "Such is life in a small town. Even two hours away, everyone knows your business."

"Would you rather be with her?" It sounded like a silly, girly question, but Kat wanted to get it out there, clear the air, and move on. She also hoped Erik would answer her honestly.

"Jesus Christ. No! That's the problem. I don't want to be with anyone else. That doesn't mean I haven't. But I constantly find myself comparing them to you... and every single one has come up short."

Hearing him talk about being with others caused jealous greed to burn, and every muscle clenched resentfully. She stopped, wrapped her arms around his neck, and pulled him down for a scalding, branding kiss. She bit his lip, marking him, making sure he knew he belonged to her, at least for this weekend.

She felt like a possessed woman, wanting to ensure she was never forgotten. She kissed a trail along the side of his scruffy jaw, relishing the telltale signs she knew it would leave on her face. Her fingers trembled as she unbuttoned his shirt, then trailed kisses down his chest, following the patches of skin revealed by the separating fabric.

A sigh escaped as she slipped the fabric from his shoulders and admired the smooth expanse of exposed flesh. She treasured the shiver that wracked his body as she licked, then nipped one of his small, pebbled nipples.

It was dark, and they'd stopped on a deserted section of beach. Taking advantage of the seclusion, she dropped to her knees and kissed a trail along his stomach as low as his clothing would allow. His shorts were tied with a drawstring, and in a matter of seconds, she'd slid them and his boxers over his hips, freed his cock, and had it wrapped in her hands.

His head dropped back and a hiss pushed through his teeth as she licked and sucked on the engorged head. Small, precisely placed flicks, licks, and swirls had his chest heaving and his hips thrusting forward. She wrapped her lips over the tip, sucking enough to tease, but not enough to satisfy.

He pushed his fingers through her hair, then grasped a fistful, trying to move her head and manipulate the speed and depth of her mouth.

Despite her greedy need to devour, she stopped and rolled her gaze up to his. Her expression let him know she was in charge, and he had no control over the speed or timing of the eventual outcome.

Through the filtered light of the moon she saw his eyes, full of heat and rampant desire. His jaw muscle flexed as he clenched his teeth and dropped his hands, putting himself in her control.

Fueled by his surrender, a deeper need erupted within her. She resumed her ministrations, combining efforts of hands, tongue, and lips. It didn't take long before he shuddered and ground out a warning. "You'd better stop. Now."

She clamped her fist tightly around the base and blew a gentle stream of air across his slick and heated flesh. When she sensed the tide receding, she started back with the sensual assault. She swirled her tongue along the most sensitive spots, then slid down the length of him until he nudged the back of her throat. Greedy and needy, she wanted all of him. She took a deep breath, relaxed her throat muscles, and continued her descent until her nose rested against his flesh and curls.

He tensed, then trembled. Struggling to hold back, he groaned. "Shit,

Kat. You're killing me."

She slowly withdrew and caught his gaze. "What did you say about an ice cream cone? Something about a lick here?" She licked underneath, from base to tip, and watched his jaw flex. "And a nibble there." She gently nipped the sensitive tip, then soothed the sting with a swirl of her tongue. "Did you mention sucking?"

As she wrapped her lips around him and took his entire length into her mouth, his control shattered. He grabbed her head and growled as she took him down her throat, continuing to suck and pull until he jerked away, too sensitive for the contact.

She dropped tender kisses along his thighs, then up his stomach to his heaving chest. One look at his face had her wanting to ask what he was thinking, but it would've been pointless. She doubted he'd be honest, even with himself. And besides, it didn't matter what he said. His expression said it all. He was as terrified as he was satisfied.

***

Erik cradled Kat's cheek in his palm and rubbed the pad of his thumb over her red and swollen lips as he sucked in cool, calming breaths. "You are amazing."

And she was tearing him from his frame.

He'd never had a blow job like that, and the thought of how she'd become so proficient at the act left him agitated. First the flowers, then Kevin, and now his growing contempt for her ex-lovers. No, he wasn't the jealous type.

Not at all.

He mentally cursed and chastised himself. He wished he could say the added sensory stimulation from the moon, wind, and waves had added to the pleasurable experience, but that wasn't it.

Emotions were coming into play, and this was transcending sex. With every touch, kiss, and incredible suck, he fell in deeper and deeper.

He recognized this particular act for what it was: a woman's need to mark her man. The scary part was, he didn't care. Hell, at this moment, if she wanted to tattoo her name on his ass, he'd go buy the fucking ink.

He retied his pants and picked up his shirt. Taking her by the hand, he headed back to the house and said, "What do you say we grab some food and take it upstairs to the deck?"

"That sounds great. Far away from the clutches of Lizbeth, I'll be safer up there."

Her tone was teasing, and he appreciated her understanding about Lizbeth, but he questioned the accuracy of her statement. "I'm not so sure that's the safest place for you. I'll have plenty of time to recover by then. You might be in serious trouble."

She smiled and batted her eyes. "I crave trouble."

After filling plates with enough BBQ, potatoes, green beans, and hush puppies to feed them for days, Erik headed to his upstairs suite with Kat close on his heels. He set the food on the deck table, then turned to go back inside for drinks and a blanket.

Kat stood in the doorway, bent over at the waist, shaking out her hair, with her dress puddled at her feet. She righted herself, and, wearing only a thong and a smile, said, "I wanted to be ready... for when you're ready."

"When it comes to you, I'm always ready."

She walked toward him with slow, purposeful strides that made her hips sway in the most hypnotic way. "Are you sure?"

Never taking his eyes off her, he slid his shorts and boxers off and sat in an Adirondack chair. Stroking his erection enticingly, he said, "What do you think?"

She was a wet dream come to life as she swayed toward him, her eyes locked on his fist, firm breasts bouncing with each step, long hair swishing across her back. Straddling him, she threaded her feet into the space between the chair and seat and lowered herself onto his lap.

Her eyes drifted closed, and she moaned as she planted her hands on his chest and scooted forward so the only thing separating them was the tiny triangle of her thong.

He held her in place at the waist and ground against her slick heat. Jesus, he was an idiot. How could he have thought he'd ever get enough of this woman?

Leaning back against the incline of his legs, she opened herself and gave him full access to her body. As he slid his palm along her slender side to the swell of her breast, she arched in a silent plea for more. He gently cupped the heavy weight in his palm, then pinched her nipple sharply.

She gasped and moaned and wiggled on his lap, trying to get closer and create more friction.

He closed his eyes and took a deep breath, forcing himself to calm before he came from nothing more than her grinding against him. He trailed his free hand along her inner thigh to the edge of her panties. Through the fabric, he worked his thumb in slow, steady circles over her clit until her body trembled, then stiffened with a fast-approaching orgasm.

When she bit down on her lip, a sure sign she was about to explode, he shoved the fabric of her panties aside and pushed into her. She cried out, then leaned forward and captured his gaze with hers. He wanted to break the connection and look away, but was trapped.

No words were spoken; they didn't need them. Her feelings were written in her expression and poured out of her with every move. Every time she impaled herself with a steady rise and fall... rise and fall... rise and fall... there was a silent *I love you* whispered in the air.

And even though the words refused to breach his lips, his body screamed them in return.

He cupped her breasts in one hand, ran his tongue along her jawline and down her collarbone, and stroked her clit with his other hand. Within moments, she fell over the edge into climactic bliss with him following right behind.

His body was still pumping into her when his blood ran cold and his heart seized with panic. He'd been so caught up in the moment, he'd forgotten a condom. Shock and disbelief tore through him. "Kat," he gasped through panic and a parched throat. "I didn't wear a condom."

She dropped her head onto his shoulder and drug in a few deep breaths of her own. "It's okay. I'm on the pill."

He grabbed her by the shoulders and pushed her back so she was at arm's length and he could see her face. "It's not okay." His rough grasp and harsh tone had her opening sleepy eyes and trying to focus on him. "It was incredibly stupid and careless of me. I swear to you I've never had sex with anyone without a condom before. I'm completely clean."

She smiled sweetly and with soft, loving strokes ran her hand down the side of his face. "I believe you. I'm clean too, so we're fine."

She rested her head on his chest and snuggled her arms around his waist. With her wrapped in his arms, listening to the thunderous roar of the waves crashing on the beach and the outrageous party going on below them, this could have been a perfect moment.

But Erik couldn't shut off his internal ramblings long enough to enjoy it.

She was the most beautiful woman in the world to him, both outwardly and inwardly. How could he not love this giving, compassionate, sensual woman?

But what would his love do to her?

Would he end up destroying her like he had Lindsey?

He had no doubts about Kat's feelings. They'd been written on her face and carried through every movement. She loved him... And that was something he couldn't tolerate.

Chapter Thirteen

Kat slid her fingers across the soft sheets, reaching for Erik. The sheets were cold. The house was still. And an all-encompassing emptiness, very different than the previous morning when she'd woken alone, grabbed her with icy fingers and pulled her into the frigid void.

She opened her eyes and searched the room, knowing she wouldn't find Erik, but needing to look anyway. As she took in the missing details—Erik's clothes, shoes and wallet—her heart closed in on itself in a belated protective measure, and cold numbness washed through her veins.

She didn't see a note, or any kind of confirmation, but deep in her soul she knew he was gone. Gone from the room. Gone from the house. And specifically, gone from her life.

She'd made a mistake by showing all of her cards last night. She loved him and she couldn't pretend otherwise. And though she wouldn't have changed it, even if she could, it had been too much for him to handle.

What frustrated her most was knowing he cared too. He, however, seemed determined to fight his feelings at all cost.

Assuming he had indeed abandoned her—at his house, no less—she should be furious. But she couldn't muster up the mad. All she felt was a heavy, gut-wrenching sadness. Sadness for him because of his obvious pain, a pain she didn't understand because he kept her locked out of that part of his life. And sadness for herself because, by loving him, she pushed him away.

She flung off the sheets with a sigh. Lying here feeling sorry for herself wasn't going to get her anywhere. She might as well face the world and figure out a way back to Riverside.

Showered and dressed, she grabbed a Diet Coke from the bedroom's mini fridge and made her way through the mess in the house and out to the deck. Steve sat in one of the Adirondack chairs, a two-liter of Coke in one hand, a bottle of Tylenol in the one with the cast. He had his baseball hat pulled low over his eyes and appeared to be sleeping. But when the french door opened, he shifted, then twisted to look at her.

"Hey," she said, dropping into the chair next to him. She propped her feet on the railing, wrapped one arm around her waist, and took a drink of her Diet Coke.

"Hey."

No "good mornings" uttered here, and she was grateful he didn't feel the need to pretend it was.

From the corner of her eye, she saw him watching her. After a few awkward moments, he adjusted his ball cap and said, "You know... technically, the sonovabitch left me."

This was painful and embarrassing and she didn't want to talk about it, but the subject couldn't be avoided. Everyone knew Erik was gone, or they would soon enough. And, on top of that, she needed someone to give her a ride back to Riverside.

She looked at Steve from the corner of her eye. "What do you mean?"

"Bastard stole my bike." He grinned as her eyes widened. "He's not a total ass. He left a note saying he wanted you to have his car to get home."

Well, that solved the problem of getting home, but... He'd left a note for Steve and not for her? "Huh. I think I might disagree with you about that total ass part."

She had a million questions about Erik's past and why he was so afraid of caring for anyone. But she didn't want to push Steve for answers, so she said nothing. She stared at the water, finding it hard to believe that everything appeared exactly the same as yesterday. The kids were splashing and playing. The waves were crashing on the shore. The seagulls were circling against a gorgeous blue sky.

But today, she was crumbling into a million pieces. It was true—the world didn't stop for broken hearts.

Whistling from the steps interrupted her pity party, and she looked in that direction to see who the next witness to her humiliation would be. When Kevin reached the top of the landing and saw Steve, he stopped in his tracks and his whistle died out in a way that would've been humorous under different circumstances.

He scanned the driveway, then looked back at Steve. "Where's your bike?"

Steve threw his hands in the air. "Beats the shit out of me."

Kevin slid his gaze to Kat as he cautiously made his way across the

126

deck.

She gave him a small finger wave and said, "Hey."

"Hi." His eyes narrowed as he glanced around, and his voice held a hard edge when he said, "Where's Erik?"

Steve did the shit-if-I-know hand toss again. "I assume with my bike."

Kevin stiffened and grew unnaturally still. His eyes darkened to almost black, and the fierceness firing from them caused a chill to creep over Kat. She made a quick mental note. *Never, ever piss off Kevin Mazze.*

He drew in a breath and, with what appeared to be great effort, relaxed his features before shifting his gaze to Kat.

Trying to sound lighthearted rather than brokenhearted, she lifted a shoulder and joked. "I guess I'm too much for him to handle."

Kevin leaned against the railing, crossed one ankle over the other, and placed his hands on the banister at either side of his hips. He studied the deck boards as if they were tea leaves, then shifted his focus to Steve.

She didn't understand the unasked question registering on his face, but apparently Steve did because he shrugged and said, "Up to ya."

"Sugar," Kevin said, then paused and took a deep breath. "I'd love to put you in my truck, take you home, and spend the rest of the day convincing you of all the ways I'm better than Erik." He winked as a wicked grin spread across his face. "And I *am* better than Erik."

Despite the tension hanging in the air and the sadness clawing at her soul, she laughed. Physically, he didn't do anything for her. But she had no problem believing, with his bodybuilder physique and his dark, assessing attitude, he was quite capable of making a woman weak in the knees.

The smile dropped from his face and he frowned. "But Erik needs you."

"Ummm… Apparently not."

"Yeah, he does." He scrubbed a hand over his face and blew out a harsh breath. "Christ, I can't believe I'm defending the dumbass, but it's obvious he cares about you. A lot. And that's the part he can't handle."

Having Kevin confirm Erik's feelings gave Kat a flutter of hope. Deep down, she knew he cared. But considering the current circumstance, she questioned whether those feelings were real, or if she just wanted it so desperately she imagined it.

He chuckled. "He called me before our first meeting and threatened to rip my heart out if I hit on you. I knew then that you were something special." His laughter built. "Damn, it was fun playing cards and drinking shots with you. He was so pissed off I thought he would pop a nut."

His laughter faded into sadness. "Erik's never run from anything in his life. The fact that he's gone now shows the magnitude of how messed up he is." He cast a quick glance at Steve before continuing. "I don't know how much he's told you about his past…"

"He hasn't told me much. I know he was almost engaged, but I don't know what happened."

His throat bobbed with his effort to swallow, and his eyes grew cloudy. "Her name was Lindsey, and it didn't end well. I don't know how he survived it. I'm not sure I would have."

She shifted her attention to Steve, who wore a solemn expression that matched Kevin's. He was staring at the ocean and seemed a million miles away.

"I've tried to get him to open up and talk to me. That's how I found out he'd been engaged… almost engaged. But when not completely shutting me out, he's been vague."

Steve shifted in his seat and cleared his throat. "Getting him to open up won't be easy. He's lived in his own personal hell for ten years. He's put down roots and gotten comfortable there."

Kevin pulled her out of the chair and wrapped her in a warm, affectionate embrace. He kissed the top of her head, and said, "We're here for you. If you need anything…" He pulled away and shrugged nonchalantly. "And I mean anything… like someone to beat some sense into Erik… just let us know." He brushed his knuckles across her cheek, and added, "Just don't give up on him. Okay?"

She smiled despite the tears rolling down her cheeks. She wasn't sure what to do to get through to Erik, but she drew courage and strength from the depth of caring these two had for him, and by transference, for her. As she fought off the suffocating despair, hope and resolve took flight in her gut.

Speaking mostly to herself, she said, "Okay. If I have to wade through hell to reach him, that's what I'll do." She winked at Kevin, then smiled at Steve. "Can I give you a ride home?"

It was hard to tell which had done more damage, the biking accident or the Southern Comfort, as he gripped the bottle of Tylenol and stood with a grunt and groan. "That'd be great. Give me ten minutes, and I'll be ready."

"Remember, sugar," Kevin said, as she opened the french door, "we're here for anything you need. Just don't give up on him."

***

Erik leaned against the old oak tree and stared at the pristinely maintained grave. Anguish and regret had been his constant companions for ten years, whether he was consciously thinking of Lindsey or not. But whenever he came here, self-loathing and hatred threatened to consume him. It had been three years since he'd made this trip, and why he had the destructive need to come at four o'clock this morning, he didn't know.

Bullshit. You know exactly why.

Yeah, because he loved Kat and was terrified of destroying her, just as he had Lindsey. He needed the physical reminder of what his kind of love did to a person.

There were a lot of things about Kat that reminded him of Lindsey: the long, black hair and green eyes, but mostly her kind and gentle nature.

Grief clogged his throat as he wondered what Lindsey would be doing right now, if she were alive. Would they have made it together this long? So many people didn't stay married anymore. Would they have been one of the lucky ones? Would she be hauling their children to soccer games or dance lessons? Would she and his mother have become friends, or at least tolerated each other? Would she have adjusted to life on the coast, after having grown up in the mountains?

She might have loved the coast, had you given her the chance to find out.

He dropped his head into his upraised hands. Sitting here, asking these unanswerable questions was pointless. All these what ifs were nothing but dead ends. The real question, the one he refused to cast a light on, was, what about Kat?

His heart begged him to get back on that bike, go back to Riverside, and grovel at her feet for being an undeserving ass. But his head screamed it would be a selfish move. He needed to stay as far away from her as possible.

Dust stung his eyes as a sudden gust of wind lashed across the cemetery. As it subsided, a slow, gentle breeze brushed his face. It felt like Lindsey's fingers as she caressed his cheek, something she did often.

He moved closer to the marker for a better look at her picture. Was her spirit here with him? If she could speak to him, what would she say?

As he stroked a finger along the picture's edge, a chill washed over his neck, and an urgent need to see her parents shook him. He dropped his hand and sighed. As much as he would love to see them, he couldn't. If he did, he would have to tell them what prompted his visit.

In the years since Lindsey's death, they'd encouraged him to move on with his life in every way and had reassured him it was okay, even healthy, for him to fall in love again.

But he'd sworn there would never be anyone else. Guilt and shame kept him from admitting he'd been wrong. Besides, there wasn't any point confessing anything to Lindsey's parents. He and Kat were finished, and that was that.

***

Kat fought a valiant battle, but feared losing the war. As she paced circles around her apartment, wondering where Erik had gone, the temptation to be miserable grew exponentially. Steve seemed to know, but would only say if his hunch was right, it would be late before Erik returned.

Moping around never fixed anything and, usually, neither did running. But it made her feel better and kept her mind occupied, so she changed into her running clothes and shoes and hit the streets. As her feet pounded the pavement, running along the waterfront, then veering off along the narrow frontage road, she considered the bits and pieces she knew about Erik.

The night they met, through subtlety and innuendos, he let her know he didn't do serious relationships. After hearing stories of his wild and crazy lifestyle, she assumed it was because he enjoyed living a free and easy, unencumbered life. However, the closer she got to him, the less certain she was. He didn't seem to embrace the lifestyle as much as he simply wanted to avoid relationships.

But why? Why had he been "almost" engaged?

Kevin and Steve made it sound as if something tragic had happened. She considered doing an internet search to see what she could find, but that felt wrong. It seemed like an invasion of his privacy, and she'd rather hear his story directly from him. She just had to figure out a way to get him to open up and let her in. If he didn't, she'd never have the chance to soothe his old wounds and help him heal.

As she rounded the final bend, almost home, her legs and lungs burned with each step. The pain was a wonderful diversion to the ache and frustration gripping her heart, and she considered going the distance again. But it was almost dark, and there were several things she needed to do for work, especially since she hadn't gone back on Thursday night as planned. With a deep breath and a final push, she sprinted the rest of the way to her apartment, hoping and praying exhaustion helped her get a decent night's sleep.

Chapter Fourteen

K at slogged into the office conference room and dropped into the chair, uninspired and as enthusiastic as she was going to get for the early Monday morning staff meeting. Everyone except Rusty was already seated, and they greeted her with a variety of nods, smiles, and what-the-hell-is-wrong-with-you expressions.

Despite pushing herself to the point of exhaustion on her run, she hadn't slept a wink. Her mind had insisted on hashing and rehashing the situation with Erik until she was physically and emotionally exhausted. Apparently, even exhaustion wasn't the magic bullet for sleeping.

Seth's shoulder brushed hers as he leaned in close and whispered, "I've seen road kill look better than you. Are you okay?"

She managed a chuckle and patted his hand. Despite his outlandish phrasing, she knew he meant well, and she appreciated his concern. Giving him a weary smile, she said, "You're a good man, Seth. Someday, you're going to make a great wife."

He rolled his eyes and tried to look put off, but the blush coloring his cheeks and the veiled gratitude in his eyes let her know he appreciated the comment.

A sound at the door caught her attention, and she turned in time to see Rusty shuffle into the conference room. Instantly, she went on high alert. Something was wrong because Rusty didn't shuffle. Ever. He always moved with zest and vigor and barely contained excitement. But today, he moved as if his feet were ten times too heavy for his legs.

He glanced around the room, seemingly to make sure everyone was accounted for. But when his gaze landed on Kat, his brow dropped slightly and an indefinable expression clouded his features. His gaze lingered on her a little longer than everyone else, and he cleared his throat before looking away.

Kat pulled out of her slump and sat straight up. She tried to regain his attention, but after his initial glance, he seemed determined to look anywhere but at her.

Her mind kicked into gear as a jolt of fear shot through her. When they'd gotten back from the beach, she and Steve had left Erik's car in his driveway. Kevin had then dropped each of them off at the respective homes, and after that, she hadn't heard from any of them.

What if something had happened to Erik? Wouldn't Steve or Kevin have called her?

As her thoughts continued to spiral out of control, Rusty started the meeting. She tried to concentrate, but the lack of sleep made her distress worse, and her attention remained divided between the meeting's conversation and thoughts of Erik.

Until Elise started talking… and key words buzzed like ringtones in the muddled fog of Kat's brain.

Brandon Kauffman

Kauffman Motors

Extensive media.

Billboards.

Elise was talking about a new business account she'd picked up over the weekend. A contact *Kat* had made last week and had an appointment with tomorrow.

Kat whipped her head around to face Elise. "You bitch!" The words, filled with all the repressed frustration and pent-up anger from the weekend, flew out of her mouth before she processed the open and close motion of her lips.

Elise froze with her eyes wide and her mouth dropped open. Someone at the table gasped, probably Seth, while Rusty turned to her, then stilled, unsure he'd actually heard Kat right.

Elise's form grew wavy from the black spots floating in front of Kat's eyes. The blood rushing through her system reached Mach three and sent her blood pressure to a potentially lethal level. She thought back to Friday morning, when she'd stood in her office and glanced around, certain someone had been in it the night before, but unable to pinpoint a specific reason for the belief.

"You took that file and those notes from my desk. I knew someone had been in my office Thursday night, but I didn't take the time to go through everything and figure out what was missing."

Rusty turned to Elise and raised an eyebrow.

Elise's face flushed with color, and a sheen of perspiration appeared on her forehead. Not quite looking at Rusty, or anyone else, she said, "I've been working on acquiring this account for weeks."

"That's bullshit. When I talked to Brandon last week, he never mentioned talking with you. I have an appointment set with him for tomorrow afternoon. If you'd been working with him, I think he would have told me. He certainly wouldn't have wasted his time making an appointment with me."

"Meeting's over," Rusty said, glancing around the conference room table. "Elise and Kat, you stay put. Everyone else, out."

The room emptied as if the place were on fire. The last one out shut the door, and as soon as the lock clicked into place, Rusty turned to Kat. "Tell me about your conversation with Brandon."

When Elise opened her mouth, he threw up a hand and gave her a look that dropped the temperature in the room twenty degrees. "You'll have your turn. In a minute."

Kat gulped at his fierce expression, even though it wasn't directed at her. She took a few deep breaths and thanked the fates that had forced her to develop the ability to reclaim her professional veneer in a matter of seconds. She also recognized that the majority of her emotional upset was with Erik, not this situation, so she forced herself to put things in their proper perspective.

Ignoring Elise, she focused on Rusty, and said, "I spoke with Brandon last week and set an appointment for tomorrow. I saw their ads in the paper and felt like they needed help. We didn't talk about a lot of specifics over the phone. It was a general cold call. But…," she turned and glared at Elise, "I'd made detailed notes of all that I would recommend. One of the items was to increase their presence through the use of billboards. Not just in Riverside, but in the surrounding markets and especially the rural areas."

She explained a few of the other specific recommendations she'd jotted down—most of which Elise had already discussed, unfortunately—then waited for Rusty to comment.

Rusty turned to Elise, who resembled a cat that'd been tossed into a full bathtub, haughty and pissed off. "I'm sure you have a different story to tell."

Elise squared her shoulders and lifted her chin. "It sounds to me like she's been reading my notes."

Rusty scrubbed a hand down his face. "I figured you'd say something like that." He tapped his pen on the table, presumably trying to figure out where to go from here. He looked as tired as she felt, and Kat regretted that he'd been drawn into the middle of Elise's bullshit.

Finally, he took a deep breath and said to Elise, "We'll talk about this more later. Right now, I have something else that I need to discuss with Kat."

Accepting the dismissal for what it was, Elise gathered her papers and left the conference room with what Kat considered to be more pride than the circumstances warranted.

But thoughts of Elise evaporated into fear as Kat studied Rusty's expression and weighed his overall demeanor. She rubbed her hands over her arms, fending off the chill, and said, "What's wrong?"

He took a deep breath, then slowly exhaled. "I got a call from Erik…"

"Is he okay?"

He huffed and slumped lower in his seat. "No, I don't think so."

Alarm shot through her. "What? Where is he?"

He grabbed her hand to keep her from jumping up and bolting for the door. "He wants me to take back his account."

Shock rocketed through her, and she collapsed like a balloon that had been hit by a blowtorch. She blinked a couple of times and shook her head, like that would suddenly clear things up for her. "I can't believe he'd do that to me."

Rusty drew in a ragged breath and shook his head, like he didn't believe it either. "I don't know what the hell happened with you two, but I can tell you this. The man I spoke with last night didn't sound anything like the Erik I know. The voice was the same, but he was a hollow shell."

She rubbed her temples, trying to make sense of the last ten minutes. Elise had broken into her office, taken her notes, and stolen a potential client out from under her. Standard operating procedure in this business. It pissed her off, but it was to be expected.

Erik, the lying bastard who promised their personal relationship wouldn't affect their professional relationship—*I promise it won't have any effect on your job*—had just sliced her open and left her bleeding on the table.

She couldn't believe he yanked his account away from her, knowing how important her career and this job were. And not only did this move affect his account, but it also took away the cross promotion she was working on with Mazze Builders and the CPA.

Hurt and betrayal knotted her gut like a Jack-in-the-box wound too tight. She needed to confront Erik before she exploded and left a mess all over everyone. If he thought he could get rid of her this easily, he needed to think again.

The hurt and betrayal quickly morphed into fury. She knew he hurt and suspected this move was a defensive one, designed to keep her at a distance so he wouldn't have to deal with his feelings for her. But she refused to let him take the chicken-shit way out.

She thought back to Steve's description of Erik living in his own personal hell, and an image of Erik wading around in misery and despair struck her. They'd asked her to not give up on him, and she'd promised she wouldn't.

Unlike Erik, she kept her promises.

She might knock him on his ass first before grabbing him by the scruff of the neck and dragging him to higher ground. But she would do whatever it took to reach him.

Because that's what you did when you loved someone.

Rusty, who'd been patiently waiting for her to reach a level state, said, "You okay?"

"I'm getting there. But I need to go see Erik."

Rusty gave a half-smile and nodded. "Good. I'm worried about him."

Rather than bee-lining for the door, she found herself sitting in the chair, thinking. Thinking about everything that had happened this morning, all that had transpired at Reynolds and Ashbury, and everything Granddad had said over the phone.

She took several deep breaths to get into her zone and carefully considered the words fighting to break free from her lips. One should never make life-altering decisions under extreme duress, but she was tired of living like this. "Rusty, I appreciate the opportunity you've given me here and have enjoyed working for you. But I need to give my two week notice. I'll have the official documentation for you this afternoon."

Rusty drew back in shock. "What?"

She reached across the table and took his hand in hers. "I don't want to be constantly looking over my shoulder, wondering where the next knife is coming from. I want to find something less cutthroat and to work someplace where I can really make a difference in people's lives."

Rusty stared at her with a blank face, seemingly at a total loss. After several moments, he squeezed her hand, then stood. "Why don't you talk to Erik and get that situation resolved." He smiled warmly. "Then we'll talk about this resignation stuff. Okay?"

By the time she walked home, got her car, and made the trek to Erik's office, an hour had passed. The time and space had been good, had given her the opportunity to calm down, soothe some of the rawness of her emotions, and figure out what to say to Erik.

She doubted Erik had thought to warn Elaina, Monteague Boats' receptionist, that a pissed-off Kat might show up on their doorstep. But just in case, she slipped on a friendly, non-threatening mask before entering the lobby. "Good morning. I need to see Erik."

Elaina didn't seem to be concerned about Kat's unstable emotional state, but she also wasn't carrying the same lightness as the day Kat toured the plant. "I'm sorry. He's not in."

Kat studied her expression for a moment and decided she wasn't covering for Erik by giving the old he's-not-available response, when he was actually hiding in his office. "Do you know where I can find him?"

Elaina chewed her bottom lip as her brow drew into a sharp V. "He hasn't been in all morning." She leaned forward and glanced down the hallway toward the suite of offices. Lowering her voice, she said, "He hasn't even called. Mr. Monteague has been trying to reach him all morning, but as far as I know, he hasn't gotten through."

Kat's anger circled the drain as concern set it. Despite her angry crack about him needing to be less of a playboy and focusing more on work, she'd come to realize he was extremely dedicated to his job and doubted this was a common occurrence. "Has he ever not shown up before?"

Elaina shook her head. "Never."

Hard to believe being abandoned at the beach could be a good thing, but Kat had just found the silver lining. Because of needing to leave his car in the driveway, she knew where he lived. "Thanks, Elaina. I'll go by his house."

***

Erik jabbed… jabbed… jabbed at the punching bag, but his muscles were exhausted from hours of rigorous exercise, and he didn't have enough strength left to make the bag move. He wrapped his arms around it and leaned against the heavy mass, relying on its weight to hold him upright.

Despite the hours of abuse he'd put his body through, he still felt the pain and agony of what he'd done to Kat. Leaving her at the beach had been low. Taking his account away from her was something only the lowest, slimiest, nastiest slug in the puddle would do.

Between that and going to Lindsey's grave yesterday, his guilt, shame, and self-loathing had reached new depths. He literally felt like he was drowning in a poisonous well.

He shoved off the bag and looked over the rest of his home gym, determined to find something that would give him relief from his all-consuming pain. What he found instead was Kat, standing in the doorway watching him.

He closed then reopened his eyes, making sure he wasn't hallucinating. Nope, she was still there, with anger and disappointment written all over her face.

The sight of her amplified his ache to the point he felt ripped inside out.

He pulled off the boxing gloves and dropped them to the floor. Grabbing a towel, he wiped the sweat from his face and neck, then grabbed a bottle of water. He was having a hard time catching his breath and gathering his thoughts, so he decided to address the fuck-ups in sequential order. "I'm sorry for leaving you at the beach." He swiped at his forehead again and dropped his head in shame. "It was a horrible thing to do."

"That's okay. Kevin was more than willing to drive me home."

He squeezed his water bottle so hard water gushed out of the open spout and over his fingers. Ignoring the liquid dripping from his knuckles, he flipped his gaze to her and saw a crack of a smile. Despite his anguish, he couldn't help but smile back at the teasing. "I had that coming."

"Yeah, you did." She moved into the weight room and glanced around. After taking stock of the machines and playing around with a few of the weights, she turned to face him. She crossed her arms over her chest and studied him with an odd combination of anger and compassion. "Why did you leave me like that?" She laughed without humor. "Gee, I guess I had it coming too, since you had to ask me that same question once." She swallowed hard and storm clouds filled her eyes. "But what I really want to know is why you yanked your account away from me. You promised my going to the beach wouldn't affect our working relationship."

He dropped onto a weight bench, propped his elbows on his knees, and let his hands fall loosely between his legs. He owed her the truth, but he couldn't bear to look at her. The disappointment in her eyes was more than he could handle.

Staring at a fleck on the tile floor, he said, "Let's start with the first one. I'm a self-absorbed prick. I needed time and space to think. It was four o'clock in the morning. I'd been awake all night, and I wasn't thinking clearly." He shook his head, utterly disgusted with himself. "As for the business side of it... I can't sit through meetings with you and not go crazy. Or cave in and beg you to give me another chance. I'm no good for you. I'll only end up hurting you... or worse. But I couldn't look you in the eyes and say it, so I took the coward's way out. All the way around, I took the coward's way out."

"What happened to Lindsey?"

The sound of her name on Kat's lips snapped his head up. "How do you know about Lindsey?"

Gently, as if approaching a wild animal, she moved across the room and knelt in front of him. "You said you'd been almost-engaged once. While trying to explain what a tough time you were having and why you'd left, Kevin mentioned her name. I put together that Lindsey must have been the one you were going to marry. But neither Steve nor Kevin would give me any details about what happened." Her voice didn't carry any accusation or incrimination, only soft compassion and concern.

He took a deep breath and squeezed his eyes shut, blocking the past as well as Kat's tenderness. He didn't want her compassion, or he'd never be able to keep her at a distance.

"Erik, I'm not leaving until we've hashed this out. And I might not leave even then. I love you."

He swallowed the compulsion to echo the words. He loved her more than she'd ever know, but he couldn't allow her to think there was a future for them when he'd never allow it.

"Tell me what happened to Lindsey."

He shook his head side to side in jerky movements. "No."

"Steve said you'd grown comfortable living in your own personal hell over the past ten years. Well, guess what? I've waded in, I'm standing neck deep in it with you, and I'm not leaving without you."

Shame stroked his skin like an old lover. "There's no savin' me, Kat. I don't deserve to be saved."

She shifted around and he thought she would stand, but instead, she flopped down on her ass and got comfortable. "I'm not going away."

"Jesus Christ." Frustration ripped out of him with the words. "You're determined to hear this, aren't you?"

"Yes."

He pushed to his feet and paced back and forth, while she calmly watched him stomp around the room like an angry bull. She was as stubborn as him, and if the situation had been reversed, he wouldn't leave either. He didn't want her to know about his past, but getting it all out might be the best thing. After hearing his story, she'd probably run from the room and out of his life without ever looking back.

"Lindsey and I started dating our sophomore year of college. We dated for two years, and in all that time, I never brought her home with me. Or introduced her to my family. It didn't matter in the beginning, but as time went on, she started pressuring me about it."

He absently punched at the punching bag. "I'd gone home with her several times, and her family was wonderful. They were kind and accepting and as good of people as you could ever meet. Nothing like my family."

Bitter resentment rose as the words flowed. "I knew my pretentious, arrogant-bitch mother would never approve of Lindsey because her family was poor. She would've gone out of her way to make Lindsey uncomfortable. In my mother's mind, Lindsey would've been on the same level as a servant. Not one of the family."

He stared off into space, remembering his thought processes and how he thought he could make it all work out. "I had the ridiculous notion that once we were engaged, or married, my mother would be more accepting. She'd see I loved Lindsey, and she wouldn't be so quick to point out the socioeconomic differences, because at that point, Lindsey would've been one of us."

He rubbed his chest, trying to alleviate the burning tension and ache, but it only intensified. Taking a deep breath, he forced himself to continue. "I had the engagement ring and planned to propose on Saturday. But on Thursday, I had to come home for a family meeting. Since it was just one night, and she didn't have class on Friday, Lindsey wanted to come too.

"I tried to tactfully explain how different her mother was from mine. My mother is judgmental and not accepting like hers. But she was too kindhearted to understand. Out of frustration, I blurted it all out in plain terms. My mother wouldn't think she was good enough for our family, and I didn't want to subject her to that."

He ground his palms against his eyes, trying to wipe away the image of Lindsey's crushed expression. "I wanted to protect her, but she didn't see it that way. She thought I was ashamed of her."

He rested his forehead against the window and stared at the river. Tears of shame and regret burned the back of his eyes, and for the first time in ten years, he couldn't stop them. "We had a huge fight... She left my apartment, hurt and angry. I was angry that she'd been difficult. But mostly, I was furious with myself for hurting her."

His sharp exhale fogged the glass, and he absently swiped his fingers through the moisture, wishing the past could be so easily erased. "I decided to take her home with me and protect her the best I could from my mother. I was determined to make her understand... it wasn't that she wasn't good enough. In reality, my family wasn't good enough for her.

"She didn't have a cell phone, so I got in my car and went after her." Tremors began in his fingers, then climbed his arms and spread through his body as he recalled the events in clear, horrifying detail. His throat closed, and he had to force the words past the blockage. "She ran a red light... I got there moments after the accident happened. People were rushing to her car, trying to help. The driver's side door had been hit, and we couldn't get to her."

He looked at the scars on his palms. "I shredded my hands trying to rip through the metal... but I couldn't get to her... There was nothing I could do. The paramedics said she died on impact, and it wouldn't have made a difference. But it would have... She wouldn't have been in that car alone."

***

Kat felt Erik's pain in every fiber of her being. She swiped her tears away and stifled a sob. She wanted to go to him, to hold him, and take away some of his pain. But she couldn't do any of that for him. He'd stuffed this down for too long, and he needed to work through it on his own terms.

Anger and outrage marred his handsome face as he turned to face her. "I allowed her to die thinking she wasn't good enough. Nothing could have been further from the truth. I, *obviously*, wasn't good enough for her. When I asked her dad's permission to marry her, I promised him I would take care of her. I failed in every possible way."

Unable to allow this faulty thinking to continue, Kat stood and closed the gap between them. "The accident wasn't your fault. She drove the car. She ran the red light." She stroked away her tears, then cupped his jaw in her palm, forcing him to look at her. "It was a horrible tragedy, but it wasn't your fault."

"Not taking her home with me. Allowing her to think, even for a second, that she wasn't good enough... that was my fault. And that's what caused the accident." Renewed determination set in as he yanked his head away from her hand. "I will never risk doing that to anyone again. Especially not you." He picked up his water bottle and tossed the towel over his shoulder. Looking at her with a mixture of regret and determination, he said, "You know the way out."

Chapter Fifteen

---

rik fought back an anguished howl as he watched Kat circle around the driveway and leave his property.

Dammit, sending her away *was* the right thing.

So why did it feel like his heart had been ripped from his chest while his soul collapsed?

The sound of the ringing phone pulled his attention away from the window. His dad, along with everyone else at the plant, must be wondering where he was, so he gave in to the incessant ringing and snatched up the receiver. "What?"

"Son? Are you all right?"

He ground his teeth together and bit back a snide remark. No, he wasn't all right. He'd never be all right again. But that wasn't his dad's fault, and there wasn't any need to take it out on him. Squelching his frustrations, he said, "I'm fine. I just had some stuff to do this morning. I need to shower, then I'll be there."

"Okay, good. When you come in, bring my golf clubs. I've got a game scheduled tomorrow."

"Will do."

He disconnected the call and headed for a much needed shower. While standing under the pulsating spray for what seemed like hours, he wished the water could also wash away all of his life's ugliness. That of the past ten years. And especially that of the past two days.

While his on-demand water heater would allow him to stay in the shower forever without running out of hot water, he couldn't hide in the tile enclosure forever. It was time to man up and face the rest of the godforsaken day.

Kat and Steve had left Erik's car in the driveway with the key under the mat, so he cut through the garage, grabbed his dad's clubs, and exited the side door. He pushed the button on his key fob to pop the trunk, and as it lifted, a flash of pink caught his attention. The sight of Kat's boogie board set off a barrage of memories that acted like an electrical shock, stopping his breath and short-circuiting his heart.

Kat wading into the ocean in running clothes, laughing and splashing with the kids.
Kat good-naturedly throwing back shots with his friends after losing in cards.
The pleasure on her face and the look in her eye when they...
Made love?

Yeah, that's exactly what it had been. Even though she hadn't said I love you until today, their connection had grown hotter and stronger until the words hadn't been necessary. He'd seen it in her eyes and it terrified him, because it forced him to acknowledge that he loved her too.

And the way he felt now was how he'd feel if something tragic happened to her. He felt a breath away from dying himself, and the reality of the situation rocked him. He wasn't being chivalrous and saving Kat from himself, although he used the bullshit excuse that she was better off without him. In truth, he was protecting himself from the risk of once again suffering a devastating loss.

And doing a piss-poor job of saving either of them. Shit, all he'd done was pile grief onto both of them.

Love had risk associated with it. But it didn't have to turn out badly. For all he knew, he and Kat might have seventy years of bliss ahead of them.

Jesus, he was a fucking idiot.

Could she ever forgive him? That seemed like a tall order, even for someone as big hearted and loving as Kat, but he had to give it a try.

However, before he could move fully forward with his life—one that hopefully included Kat—he had to forgive himself for the past. He dumped the clubs in the trunk of his car, then ran back inside. He had a call to make.

***

After talking with Lindsey's parents for an hour, Erik felt like he'd been drug across the Atlantic behind a freighter. He shed ten years' worth of tears and purged the deep regret he harbored. He told her parents about Kat and all the ways she reminded him of Lindsey. The important ways, like her big heart, compassionate nature, and ability to see beyond people's faults and love them anyway.

And he promised to introduce them to Kat as soon as he worked this whole mess out.

After a quick call to his dad to say he wasn't going to make it to work after all, he ran down the pier, jumped on his boat, and headed across the river.

As he crossed the street to SMG, Rusty exited the front door. Seeing Erik, he stopped on the steps and waited. "You all right?"

Erik smiled. He must look like hell, but on the inside, he couldn't remember being better. "Yeah, I am. But I'll be even better after I see Kat." He started to pass Rusty on the steps, then paused and said, "Oh… you're fired. I want Kat back."

His laughter and elevated mood died when Rusty said, "She's not here. And you can't have her back; she quit."

"What?" He backed down the step to stand even with Rusty.

Rusty shrugged. "I told her I wouldn't accept her resignation in the heat of the moment, but I'm not counting on a change of heart. Between you and Elise, I think she's done."

Erik scrubbed a hand over his head. "I fucked up. I know it. But I'm here to apologize and make things right. Both personally and professionally…" The sentence died off as Rusty's words sank in "What did Elise do?"

"Same old bullshit." He threw up a hand and shook his head. "I don't want to talk about it. And you need to find Kat. Last I saw her, she was headed off to find you." He shrugged. "I haven't seen her since, so I'd check her house."

After ringing the doorbell and knocking several times, Erik decided Kat's house was too still for her to be home. But her car was in the lot, so where could she be?

Running.

One thing he learned about her over the weekend was that she ran when stressed. And thanks to the way he treated her, her stress level was probably pretty damned high. He took a seat on the deck overlooking the waterfront and got comfy. He didn't care how long he had to wait; he wasn't going anywhere until he had the chance to apologize.

Thirty minutes later, he saw a lone figure jogging along the narrow road paralleling the river. He could tell she'd been running a long time by her labored strides and slow pace, and he wished for the hundredth time today he could kick his own ass.

With each step she took, his doubt grew stronger. What if she wouldn't forgive him for being an asshole? What if he hurt her so badly she *couldn't* forgive him?

He brushed the doubt aside, refusing to accept the negative thoughts. Hoping to shake off his explosive nervous energy, he paced back and forth on her deck and watched her draw near.

She ran facing traffic, and several cars were coming from behind. He checked his watch and noted the high school had just let out, which explained the heavy traffic on this normally sparsely traveled road.

Suddenly, a dog ran out from the brush. It barked at Kat and ran across the road, chasing her. The lead car slammed on brakes and avoided hitting the dog. But the second car in line didn't brake, and instead, swerved to keep from rear-ending the car in front.

As it crossed the center of the road and headed straight for Kat, a panicked warning ripped from his throat. But Kat was too far away to hear him over the squealing tires and blaring car horns.

Kat turned her head and looked behind her as the swerving car slammed on brakes, but it was too late.

The car hit her with a sickening thud and tossed her into the air like a ragdoll.

Shock and horror ripped through him, buckling his knees and freezing his lungs, as Kat's lifeless body rolled once, then stopped facedown on the grass. Reflexes took over, and without conscious thought, Erik had his cell phone in his hand, dialing 911 while running down the stairs when he heard sirens approaching.

Kat's apartment was in the old fire station, and the new station had been built next door. The crewmen were always sitting in the doorway, watching the traffic, and must have seen the accident occur. By the time he reached Kat's side, the paramedics had also arrived. Matt Vickers, a Riverside resident Erik had known all of his life, was the lead paramedic. He and Erik pushed through the crowd and reached her side at the same time.

Erik swallowed the terror in his throat and beat back the rising bile to ask, "How bad does it look, Matt?"

"Do you know her?"

Unable to speak around his closed throat, Erik nodded.

"It's hard to know exactly what we're dealing with. Right now, we've got a pulse, and although it's unsteady and labored, she's breathing on her own."

Erik shook from head to toe as adrenaline ripped through his system. The numbness in his extremities began to recede as they put her in a neck brace, then gingerly placed her onto a backboard.

"I'm going with her." This was nonnegotiable, and he hoped he didn't have to throw down in the street with Matt to make it happen.

Matt nodded. "You'll have to ride in the front." As the other paramedics placed Kat in the ambulance, Matt asked, "Do you know her next of kin?"

Paralyzing fear locked him in place and froze his breathing.

His expression must have screamed his panic because Matt placed a reassuring arm on his shoulder and said, "We just need to notify her family of the accident."

Relief flooded his system and made him weak-kneed again, but he somehow managed to stay vertical and get his faculties working. He found her cell phone lying on the ground and snatched it up. "She'd want her grandfather notified first. I've never met him, but I want to be the one to call. I'll do it on the way to the hospital."

The next several hours passed in a blur. The doctor said although her injuries weren't life threatening, they were extensive and severe. Erik lost track of the broken bones and scrapes and concentrated on the biggies. Broken ribs had punctured a lung, and there was significant head trauma. Because of that, they would keep her heavily sedated and intubated for several days. They also wouldn't know if there was permanent brain damage until she'd regained consciousness.

For the first time in years, Erik closed his eyes and prayed.

***

Around midnight, Kat's parents and grandfather arrived. Erik introduced himself as a friend of Kat's, and soon after their arrival, the doctor came in to explain the situation.

Kat's grandfather asked questions while her father sat quietly in a chair. Her mother paced the room in her tailored suit and conservative one-inch heels, appearing more agitated and inconvenienced than concerned. As soon as the doctor left the room, Kat's mother said, "Well, there isn't a need for us to stay here any longer tonight." Turning her attention to Erik, she said, "I noticed several hotels around the hospital. Is this a decent area? Can you suggest a suitable hotel?" Without giving Erik a chance to respond, she waved her hand dismissively, and said, "Never mind. I'll ask at the information desk in the lobby."

Erik stood, dumbfounded and angered by the woman's lack of concern. Kat's grandfather had been the only one to approach Kat's bed. Initially, Erik thought maybe her parents were in shock and overwhelmed and just hadn't known what to do. Now he wasn't so sure.

Her grandfather, sitting on the edge of the bed holding Kat's hand, seemed less inclined to leave. "We jus' got here. Don't ya think we should stay a while?"

Kat's mother pressed her lips together and crossed her arms. "Whatever for? The doctor said she won't be awake for days. What's the point of staying here? We've had a long drive, and I need sleep. I have an early morning conference call."

Holy shit. Erik never would've believed it possible, but Kat's mother was cut from the same bad cloth as his, maybe even worse. How could she be more concerned about a conference call than her daughter, who was lying in a hospital bed in a coma? Now wasn't the time to point out what a bitch Mrs. Owens was, but Erik filed the incident away for the future.

Kat's grandfather remained uneasy, but agreed. "I guess I'll be more use to Katydid rested than dead on my feet." He wrapped Kat in a gentle hug, then stood to address Erik. "Young man, I assume yer not leavin'?"

"No, sir."

He gave Erik's arm a reassuring squeeze, and said, "Then I'll see ya bright an' early in the mornin'."

***

True to his word, Kat's grandfather arrived at the hospital a few minutes before seven. "I woulda been here sooner, but it took me longer to walk from the hotel than I'd expected. Guess I'm not as fast as I used to be."

Disgust that the older man had to walk filled Erik as he sat upright in the recliner, then stood to shake her grandfather's hand. "Good morning, sir. I'm sorry you had to walk." His annoyance with Kat's parents was evident in his tone, and her grandfather smiled while squeezing his hand.

"I coulda insisted on a ride, but sometimes it's easier to leave well enough alone."

Kat's grandfather sat in the chair next to her bed and studied the various tubes and wires trailing to the machines scattered around her. The ventilator made a steady whooshing sound, and several monitors beeped and occasionally pinged. Overnight, Erik had grown accustomed to each of the sounds, and knew it would take her grandfather a while to do the same.

After several minutes, he turned his attention to Erik. "You the young man that took my Katydid to the beach?"

Erik smiled, wondering what Kat thought of being called a bug. "Yes, sir."

"Thanks for that. She works too hard. Those parents of hers have always made her feel like she didn't measure up. But lately, she's spent too much time tryin' to prove 'em wrong and not enough time makin' herself happy."

Guilt had Erik diverting his gaze. He sure as shit hadn't done much to make her happy over the last forty-eight hours. He sat here all night, beating himself to a bloody, emotional pulp for doing exactly what he most feared.

Hurting her.

If he hadn't been such an asshole, she would've been at his house, wrapped up safe and sound with him in his bed, rather than out running.

He shuddered as he considered how close he came to losing her. And if he had, she would've died just like Lindsey—thinking he didn't love her.

But by the grace of God, Kat had been spared, and he wasn't leaving this room until he told her how much he loved her, and how sorry he was for hurting her. He'd spend the next twenty years on his knees, begging her forgiveness, if that's what it took.

"Good morning, gentlemen."

Startled by the appearance of Daniel Sturgis in Kat's doorway, Erik jumped. He was so lost in thought, he forgot he and Kat weren't alone in the world.

After looking over Kat's chart and checking the monitors, Daniel— who Erik assumed was the day-shift neurologist—said, "She's doing fine.

She's stable and recovering exactly as we'd expect. But we're still going to keep her heavily sedated, basically in a coma, for several days to allow the swelling in her brain to recede."

"Thank you for takin' such good care of my Katydid." The old man's eyes clouded as he gazed at Kat's still form. "I don't know what I'd do without her."

"Yes, sir. I'm sorry to have to do it, but I'm glad to be here for her." He turned his attention to Erik. "You look like hell."

Erik chuckled. "Awww... Daniel, you say the nicest things. You have an outstanding bedside manner."

The doctor laughed, then grew serious. "Erik, she's not going to be alert for several more days. The nurses said they've tried to get you to go eat, or even just walk around, but you refuse to leave." The corner of his mouth lifted in a smirk. "Lots of hearts breaking out there in that nurse's station, by the way."

Erik laughed, then settled his gaze back on Kat.

"Her grandfather's here with her," Daniel continued. "You should go home, get some rest, get something to eat. Take a shower."

"I appreciate the concern, but no can do."

Daniel crossed his arms over his chest and leaned against the doorframe. "I could order you to leave."

Erik cut his gaze to Daniel and narrowed his eyes. They went to school together most of their lives, and as life in a small town would have it, spent a lot of time hanging out with the same crowd. They weren't close friends, but they knew each other well enough. "I wouldn't advise it," Erik said, making sure Daniel knew he wouldn't be swayed.

Daniel sighed and looked at Kat's grandfather. "I've known Erik long enough to know I'm fighting a losing battle and asking you to do the same. But if you can, get him to leave, at least for a little while." Speaking to both men, he said, "This isn't a sprint. Her recovery is going to be a marathon, and you're not going to do her any good if you're exhausted."

Kat's grandfather nodded.

Erik said, "Understood."

When the doctor left, her grandfather said, "He's right, ya know. I didn't wanta leave last night, but I knew it was for the best."

"I can't leave until..." He paused, swallowed, and tried again. "I have to be here when she wakes up. I have some things to tell her."

The older man studied Erik for the longest time, then smiled, giving Erik the impression he passed some kind of test. "Stubborn. That's good. Katy needs someone as strong willed and determined as she is."

The two men spent the next several hours talking and getting to know each other, while staring at Kat and wishing they could do something to change the situation. Midmorning, her parents arrived. Kat's mother was dressed in another power suit. Her father was dressed slightly more casual.

Granddad, as Erik had been instructed to call him, filled Kat's parents in on the doctor's course of action.

Kat's mother sighed and rolled her eyes. "Well, she's certainly made a mess of things this time."

Erik, dozing in and out of sleep in the recliner, became instantly alert. The tone, the words, everything about Kat's mother's statement flew through him like a wildfire out of control. But before he could get out of the chair and onto his feet, Kat's grandfather said, "What's that supposed to mean?"

Kat's mom huffed in disbelief. "I have to state the obvious? She moved to this nothing town at the edge of the earth and got herself hit by a car. She's going to be in the hospital for who knows how long, and then it'll take months for her to fully recover. She can't possibly take care of herself, let alone work, so we're going to have to move her back to Charlotte with us." She made an it's-all-so-obvious expression. "Like I said, she's certainly made a mess of things."

Color rose high in Granddad's cheeks and his breathing grew labored as he glanced at Kat. He and Erik had a lengthy conversation about how much Kat might be able to hear, and Erik knew the old man was concerned about her hearing this bullshit.

Having heard enough himself, Erik kicked the footrest of the recliner down and stood. "I'll take care of her."

Kat's mother swung her condescending gaze to him. "Excuse me?"

He loved Kat, and if she'd have him, he intended to marry her. The vows he hoped to take included for better or worse, in sickness and in health. He hadn't said them to her yet, but he felt them nonetheless. And he'd start acting on them now.

However, before he could explain any of that, Kat's mother turned her back on him and resumed her verbal tirade. "She's always been so irresponsible." She turned on Granddad. "This happened in the middle of the day. Why wasn't she at work?"

A growl built in the back of Erik's throat, but Granddad was quicker with the attack. "Leah, you're my only child, and I love ya. But I don' know where your mother and I went wrong. I thought we raised ya to be a good and caring person. I thought wrong."

Kat's mother bristled, but quickly regained her composure. "What are you babbling about?"

"Somewhere along the lines, your priorities got all outta whack. Katy's lyin' there in a coma, and you've been back at the hotel on the phone. You're complainin' because her condition is an inconvenience for ya. The only thing that oughtta matter is her. But you're so wrapped up in yourself, you can't see that."

Granddad's misty gaze shifted to Kat. "She's spent so many years tryin' to please ya and make ya happy that she's made herself miserable. You've criticized her work with charities and the animal shelter. But ya know what? I'm more proud of her for being selfless than I could ever be of you, and all that you've accomplished through your selfishness."

He turned to Kat's father, who stood off to the side looking like he'd rather eat a pile of nasty gym socks than be in this room. "Get my daughter outta here. Take her back to Charlotte." He swung his gaze around to Erik, and said, "This fine young man and I can take care of Katy without ya."

Kat's mother glared at her father. "She's obviously going to be out of work for a while. Are you going to take care of the hospital bills? Are you going to let her move in with you?"

Erik stepped up next to Granddad. "I will."

"Oh, really?" Her disgust over the situation came pouring out in those two little words. "After knowing my daughter for no more than a few weeks, you're willing to take full responsibility for her?"

For the first time in his life, Erik was grateful he'd been birthed to a mother who was also a first-rate bitch. Kat's mother, no doubt, expected Erik to shrivel under her harsh glare and scolding tone. But he had years of practice dealing with a woman like her, and he wasn't the least bit phased. "Yes, ma'am, I am. And if she'll have me, I'll happily spend the rest of my life taking care of her."

The woman snorted. "You're obviously as much of a dreamer as Katherine if you think you know her well enough, after two weeks, for that kind of commitment." She flicked a glance to her father, then to Kat, and finally to her husband. "I guess we're no longer needed here. We can go pack our things and get on with our lives."

The silence was deafening as Kat's parents gathered their briefcases and left the room. As the door shut behind them, Granddad turned to Erik. He drew in a deep breath, stood a little taller, and years melted off his face. "That felt kinda good. I shoulda done that twenty-five years ago."

He stepped over to the bed and took hold of Kat's hand. "Her mama's right; she is gonna need someone to take care of her. Katy said she thought I'd like livin' here, so I reckon I'll find out."

Erik smiled and said, "My house just happens to have a guesthouse. Consider it yours."

Chapter Sixteen

Three days turned into four and then into five. Each time they reduced the sedation, she fought the ventilator tubing so badly they had to increase it again. Because of the damage to her lung, they needed to keep her on the ventilator longer than normal, which Erik understood. But watching her struggle and fight it pushed the limits of his already taxed sanity.

He had agreed to share Granddad's hotel room... sort of. Granddad spent his days at the hospital, but stayed in the hotel at night. Erik used the room for showers. He refused to leave Kat for more than the thirty minutes it took to run to the hotel, shower, and get back. The nursing staff had come to accept him as a useless, bulky piece of equipment that needed to be worked around.

Kevin and Steve brought him clean clothes and kept him fed, and for the first few nights, alternated staying at the hospital with him. Finally, on the fifth day, he convinced them Little Bit needed the attention more than he did and would really appreciate the company.

Seth and Rusty stopped by several times throughout each day, and Elise had shown up once. She seemed truly shaken by Kat's condition and had tried to offer words of solace to Erik. Although she seemed genuine in her concern, Erik found himself standing between her and Kat, like a man protecting vulnerable prey from a vulture, just waiting to swoop in and finish the kill.

On the sixth day, they had a breakthrough. As they eased the sedation, panic once again settled around Kat. But this time, at the sound of her grandfather's voice, she flickered her eyes and followed the sound until she found him standing by her bed.

Her fight or flight reflex was strong, but she eventually followed his command to relax and gave up the fight. They still didn't know the long-term effects of the head trauma, but her ability to understand and follow Granddad's commands made everyone hopeful.

Kat slept more than she was awake for the next two days, which made it easy for Erik to stay out of sight. Because there were still questions about what she would know and remember when fully conscious, he felt it best to stay hidden to prevent any additional stress on her. Granddad didn't know the details, but knew Erik and Kat had been "arguing," and that's why she'd been running. Because of that, he was content to be Kat's focal point each time she roused.

Around two in the morning of the eighth day, Erik had his head resting on his arms on the edge of Kat's bed, drifting in and out of sleep. As he slipped deeper into that in-between state, the most magnificent dream began to unfold.

Kat's weak fingers drifted across his hand, then sifted through his hair and settled on his scalp. The effort exhausted her and she drifted back to sleep with her hand resting on top of his head. Several foggy moments later, Erik's brain cells fired, and he realized it hadn't been a dream.

Kat had reached out to him.

He snapped his head up and in the process woke her. His heart pounded in triple time, and his breath rushed out as she cracked open her eyes and settled her gaze on his face.

God, did she recognize him? Had she known it was him lying on her bed, or had she simply been trying to figure out who the mysterious person was?

He smiled and said, "Hey. Welcome back."

Earlier in the day, her Glasgow Coma score had been high enough for the doctor to remove the ventilator. Despite the balm Erik had been applying, her lips were dry and chapped, and she licked at them several times. She tried to speak, but couldn't get the words past her parched throat.

He siphoned a small amount of water into a straw, and said, "Open up. I'll drizzle a little water into your mouth."

It took a lot of effort for her to swallow. But as soon as the liquid was down, she opened her mouth like a tiny bird, eager for more. He grinned and refilled the straw. He was so glad to see her awake and responding, he would've been happy to sit there, feeding her water one straw-full at a time, forever.

After repeating the process several times, she whispered, "Thanks." Weak and barely audible, it was the most beautiful sound he ever heard.

There were so many things he wanted to say, but all of it would probably overwhelm her. Not even entirely sure she recognized him, he decided to stuff his emotional needs. Hopefully, he would have all the time in the world to shower her with I'm-sorrys and I-love-yous. But for now, his primary concern was making sure she was comfortable.

He also needed to call Granddad. Even though she had sporadic lucid moments over the past several days, this was the first time she was alert enough to speak.

"Your granddad's at the hotel getting some sleep. I need to call him and let him know you're awake."

When he reached for the phone, she rested her palm on his wrist. She looked at the phone and shook her head no, then whispered, "Glad you're here."

Extreme joy and nauseating remorse swamped him. She knew him. But he also had the sense she remembered the way he treated her. He blinked to stop the burn in his eyes, but kept his gaze locked on hers as he ran a thumb over her cracked lips, then across her cheek. "I'm so damned sorry, Kat." He took her hand in his and decided to let it all pour out. He'd rather overwhelm her with love than leave her doubting for one more second. "I love you more than anything in this world. I'll never be able to tell you how sorry I am for the way I treated you."

"I know."

Unsure if he heard correctly, he said, "You know?"

"I know… you love me. I prayed…" She licked her lips and swallowed. "I didn't want you… to go through that again."

His breath left in a whoosh and he dropped his head to the bed. He didn't know when she had that thought, but with all that she'd been through, how could he have been her concern? There were a million thoughts zinging around in his brain, but one kept jumping to the forefront. "How in the hell did I get so lucky? I don't deserve you."

She smiled faintly. "Thank you… for taking care… of me." Her eyes drifted shut as she murmured, "I love you," then went back to sleep.

The words had been barely audible, but he felt them as plainly as if they'd been screamed at the top of her lungs. "I love you, Kat. And I swear to you, I will spend the rest of my life making sure you never doubt that. Not for one second."

***

Kat didn't know how many days she'd been out of it, but it must have been a lot. Once she understood the need for the ventilator, she discovered sleep was her new best friend. It provided the escape she needed to make the tubing tolerable, and her aching body had been more than happy to cooperate.

Granddad and Erik had also been more at ease while she slept, so even if awake, she pretended to keep sleeping. After listening to their conversations for several cycles, she figured out their routines. Granddad stayed with her during the day, but went to a hotel to sleep at night. Erik went to the hotel to shower, but was never gone for long. Aside from that brief trip each day, he refused to leave her room.

At first, she was confused about where she was and what had happened. But as she listened to their conversations, the pieces fell into place until she eventually had the entire puzzle. She could tell Erik had so many regrets and kept beating himself up, and she didn't want that for him. But communicating with the ventilator in place was nearly impossible, so she waited until they removed it and her grandfather had left before reaching out to him.

There were so many things she wanted to say to him, but their brief conversation exhausted her, and it was pointless to try and get more out of her body at the moment. Rather than fight it, she let Erik's words settle around her like a comfortable blanket and fell back into the void of sleep.

Two days later, they moved Kat to a step-down unit and her hospital room became as cramped and lively as Erik's house had been during his Saturday night party. She learned her parents had gone back to Charlotte, upon Granddad's urging. And, much to her delight, she learned Granddad would be living in Erik's guesthouse to help care for her while she recuperated.

During a brief lull in visits, Kat reached for Erik's hand and said, "How is Granddad going to get from your house to my house every day?"

Erik's smile was like a jolt of electricity to her system, lighting her up from the inside out. "He'll walk across the patio and in the back door." At her arched brow, he said, "Oh, have I forgotten to tell you that I've had some of your things moved to my house?"

She laughed, then instantly regretted it as her fractured rib and broken clavicle made their presence known. "Yeah, I think you did."

"Huh…" He rubbed his hand along his jaw and chewed on the inside of his cheek, deep in thought. After several minutes, his expression grew serious and he scooted forward to the edge of his chair. "I can think of a million better places and ways to do this, but I can't think of a better time." He took her hand in both of his and stared into her eyes. "Will you marry me? We can wait as long as we need for you to be fully recovered, but I want you to know how serious I am—about you, how much I love you, and my intentions to take care of you. Not just while you're in the hospital, but forever."

Despite the busted rib and injured lung, Kat's chest expanded with joy and love. She believed he was serious, but she had one lingering question that needed to be answered before she agreed. "You're not asking out of a sense of responsibility or regret for what happened, are you?"

"No. Absolutely not. I was there… when you had the accident." He winced and hunched over as if in pain. "I was on your deck, waiting for you to come home. I intended to tell you then how much I love you. And eventually get to this step. This is not because of the accident. This is because I'm the luckiest guy in the world to have found you, and I'm making sure you don't get away from me again."

A noise at the door had both of them looking that way. Rusty had stopped midstride, and was in the process of pivoting. "Uhhh… I'm interrupting a moment. I'll come back."

"No. Well, yeah." Guarding her torso, she laughed. "But I want to talk to you. Could you wait outside for a minute while I give Erik an answer to this important question?"

Without another word, Rusty slipped out of the room and around the corner.

Feeling like she could pop with joy, Kat said, "Yes! I love you… I have since the night we met…," she leaned in close and whispered, "…and you did that thing with your tongue."

Erik laughed loud and deep and she fell a little deeper. "Now, I have a question for you."

"Okay."

"Given this new turn of events, I guess you'd be okay with me handling your account again."

He lowered his gaze and tilted his head away from her. After several muttered curses, he said, "I have so many things to apologize for."

"No, no apologies. I just… well, I've been thinking, and I'd really like to continue handling yours and Kevin's account. That is, if Rusty's in agreement with me working part time and only handling those accounts."

"Is that really what you want? You don't have to work at all and can do all the volunteering you want."

"If I'm working part time, I'll still be able to volunteer. And I really want to oversee this project with the CPA."

Erik kissed her long and hard. "Then that's what you'll do."

"Thank you. Do you mind getting Rusty for me?"

"Not at all. How about I get a pizza while you're talking with him, and we'll celebrate."

"Oh, my God. That would be amazing." Kat cut her eyes to the leftover mashed potatoes, soup, and roll from lunch. "Do you think they'll let me eat something good for a change?"

Erik grinned. "Sure. Especially if they don't know about it."

With another quick kiss, he was off, and Rusty took a seat in what she'd come to think of as Erik's recliner. "You scared us." Erik had told her that Rusty and Seth visited daily, and it was obvious from his tone and expression Rusty had truly been worried about her condition.

"Thanks for coming to check on me so often. It means a lot to know how much you care."

"When do you think you'll go home?"

Kat pushed herself into a more upright position, then caught her breath as everything settled into place. "Maybe tomorrow. If not, then definitely the next day."

He cleared his throat and grinned. "Sooo… did I really walk in on Erik popping the question?"

"Yeah, you did." She laughed, then coughed. The doctor said the coughing would continue for a while, but she hoped like hell he was wrong… It hurt like a bitch. "He should've shut the door if he wanted privacy. I'm glad you're here. I was thinking about calling you."

"Oh yeah?" He leaned forward in the recliner and rested his forearms on his knees.

"I was wondering if I could rescind my resignation. Well, partially rescind it."

"In what way?"

"I'd like to keep Erik and Kevin's accounts and work the cross promotion with the CPA. It's going to take a while for me to get back to full strength, but if those are the only two accounts I'm handling, I can easily work those from home." She grinned. "I don't think either of the clients would mind if I did that."

He laughed and relaxed back in the chair. "But those are the only two accounts you want?"

She nodded. "Yeah. I enjoy the challenge of creating effective promotions, but I'm tired of the political nastiness. Those two accounts are safe. I don't have to worry about Elise going after either of them. I mean, she can try, but Kevin and Erik won't let her within ten miles of their accounts, so I'm not concerned about that."

"Elise won't be a problem." His tone was harsh and carried an edge, and she wondered what had happened with Elise and the Kaufmann Motors account. Seeing her unasked question, Rusty said, "I think Elise has had a change of heart about you. I know she's had a change of heart about the way she handled things."

Kat grinned. "Did this change of heart happen on its own, or did you have something to do with it?"

A funny expression crossed his face, and he shrugged. "A little of both." His voice was no longer harsh, but soft and kind of sultry, and his body language...

Could they...

Rusty and Elise...

A couple?

She thought about it a few minutes, trying it on for size, and decided it wasn't out of the question. However, she didn't want any details if that's what was cooking, so she switched the subject back to something more comfortable. "So, are you okay with me working part time, on just those two accounts?"

Rusty shrugged. "I'd like for you to come back full time once you're able, but yeah, I'll take whatever I can get." He grinned. "Maybe I can gradually get you back to full time."

"Don't count on it. But I appreciate you working with me."

"I suppose you'll need time off for a wedding?" He sounded annoyed, but the grin on his face indicated he was anything but.

"Yeah, I guess I will. I think I'd like something low key and informal."

"I think that sounds perfect."

"Yeah… me too."

Later that evening, while eating their pizza, Kat, Erik, and Granddad made plans for an informal wedding at Erik's house along the banks of the Pamlico River. They would invite only close friends and family—whether or not they'd invite mothers was questionable.

After Granddad left for the hotel, Kat said, "If you got up here in bed with me, how well do you think we'd sleep?"

Erik laughed. "It would be the best night's sleep I've had in weeks." He crawled in next to her, tucked her next to his side, and kissed the top of her head. "Good night, Katydid. I love you."

Epilogue

Three months later

Kat sat on the pier, watching Erik's boat close in. He seemed to be running faster than normal, and she wondered why the rush. As he approached the pier, rather than pulling into the boathouse like normal, he pulled alongside and motioned excitedly. "Come on, get in."

"Get in? Where are we going?"

His grin was ear to ear, and his eyes were positively sparkling when he took off his sunglasses. "It's a surprise. But if you don't hurry up, you'll miss it."

Moving as quickly as possible, given she still lacked full mobility, she climbed aboard with Erik's help, then settled onto the padded seat he installed for her. As soon as she was situated, he pulled away from the pier, gave the boat full throttle, and headed back across the river.

They were almost to the middle when Kat saw them... three porpoises jumping and splashing, headed out toward the Sound.

As Erik approached, he decreased his speed, then set the boat to idle. As always, the creatures turned toward his boat and began their dance.

Erik helped Kat out of her seat, then grabbed the hem of her top and stripped it off over her head. "Hey," she said, playfully swatting at his hands. "What are you doing?"

He gave her a quick kiss and smiled broadly. "You wanted to swim with them, so we're going swimming." His eyes grew dark and heavy lidded. "I've been thinking. In the water, with buoyancy on our side, we might be able to start our honeymoon."

She didn't need to hear the suggestion twice or need further encouragement. Despite her repeated attempts to consummate their marriage, Erik had been so afraid of hurting her that cuddling and snuggling was as close to sex as they'd gotten.

Moving slowly and gingerly, she undressed Erik while he undressed her. It would have been easier and more efficient to take off their own clothing, but she missed these moments of intimacy with him and didn't want to rush.

As she stared at his naked form, nervous excitement rippled through her. It had been a long time since they'd been together, and if it took getting in the water for Erik to make love to her, she'd stay there until she was as shriveled as a hundred-year-old prune.

She just hoped the porpoise weren't under age, because they were about to get quite a show.

Excerpt - LAST CALL

Book #2 in the Heat Wave Series

The Heat Wave series books are loosely connected stories that all take place in coastal locations, mostly in North and South Carolina. The characters in Book #1 are different than those in Book #2, but in Book #3 there will be a merging of the two that will continue throughout the series.

Chapter One

G avin McLeod turned into the Blackout Bar and Grill's gravel parking lot, whipped his SUV into the first available parking space, and slammed the shifter into park. The vehicle was still rocking from the abrupt stop when he shoved the door open and stepped out into the crisp evening air.

His chest expanded as he drew the heavy salt air into his lungs, then let the explosive tension trapped in his head and neck escape on a sharp exhale. The hour-long drive from Myrtle Beach to Anticue would have been a relaxing trip, had it not been filled with constant chatter and relentless questions from his three female companions. Finally free of the confining vehicle, he took a moment to let the peaceful calm of Anticue Island seep into every cell of his body.

He hadn't been to the island in… Damn, had it really been fifteen years? The Blackout Bar and Grill was a new addition, and the old fishing pier next door was closed. But other than that, nothing about the island seemed to have changed.

The back doors of the SUV opened, and two-thirds of the troublesome trio climbed out. Their four-inch spiked heels dug into the loose, sandy gravel, pitching them off-kilter, sending them to and fro. Too far away to grab either of them, Gavin held his breath and hoped for the best. Each girl put a hand to the side of the vehicle to gain her balance, then used the car as a handrail as they made their way to the ballast-stone sidewalk.

The other one-third of his problem—which accounted for two-thirds of his headache—remained in the passenger seat. If this were a date, he would open the door and help her from the car like the gentleman his grandfather raised him to be. If it were a platonic, non-forced date with a friend, he still would help her from the car.

But this wasn't a date. And he'd be damned if he'd do *anything* to give the impression he was okay with Max and Callie's plan of manipulating him into pretending it was. In fact, Gavin was so annoyed with Max, he was thinking of demanding an increase in his profit sharing to cover his escort fee.

He stepped in front of the car, slipped his hands into his front pockets, and waited. He would prefer to walk away and leave her sulking, but he couldn't hit the lock button on the key fob until she gave up her petulance and opened the damned door.

As Jen and Tiffany teetered along the uneven stepping-stones leading to the bar's side entrance, he took in the details of the building and surrounding property. Weathered clapboard siding hung like sagging skin on a decrepit skeleton, but bright, lime-green trim gave the place a shot of vibrant color, which made the battered siding seem less tired.

Wrought iron benches, brightly painted Adirondack chairs, and copper yard ornaments created a profusion of color along the sidewalk. Hand-painted price tags hung from each piece, letting visitors know they, too, could have a bit of Anticue in their own backyard.

A smile tugged at the corner of his mouth as his gaze settled on a copper windmill. His grandfather would love the controlled chaos created by the bright colors and whimsical atmosphere of the Blackout. He would especially love that windmill.

The stone sidewalk continued past the side entrance to a front patio and balcony that overlooked the beach. During summer months, the pink, blue, and teal tables would be filled to capacity, but on this early May evening, they sat empty.

His gaze shifted to the deserted fishing pier next door, and his smile faded. He and his grandfather had spent many days tossing hooks there, and heavy sadness filled his chest at seeing it abandoned and left to the mercy of the beach's harsh elements.

Tired of waiting, he peered at Callie through the windshield and cocked an eyebrow, his message loud and clear. *Are you coming or not?* When she stuck her lip out even further and crossed her arms, he gave her a suit-yourself shrug and turned toward the entrance.

From the corner of his eye, he saw her shoulders slump in defeat. She grabbed her purse from the floor of the SUV, pulled the lever to release the door, and shoved against it with a huff. "A gentleman would have opened the door for me."

Gavin smiled and kept walking. Maybe if he turned into a first-rate asshole, he'd finally drop off Callie's radar. God knows, reasoning with her hadn't worked. Neither had the direct approach: I'm. Not. Interested.

166

All she'd ever seen was his refined business persona. She had no idea the real Gavin, buried beneath the expensive Italian suits, even existed. Maybe knocking some of the polish off his redneck would be the answer to getting her to drop her obsession.

Her friends were perched on wooden chairs at a high pub table, looking around expectantly for a waiter. Out of the ten or twelve people scattered around the bar, none looked too interested in jumping to meet the girls' demands.

The front wall that faced the beach was actually two large doors that could be rolled out of the way to create one large space between the inside and outside deck. At the back of the room sat the L-shaped service bar. One end stopped short of the kitchen entrance, while the other hooked back to the wall. Two older salts sat on bar stools at the hooked end, sipping their beers and talking.

One side of the room held a pool table, while a jukebox sat in the middle of the building, wedged against the center support beam. The rest of the area was filled with an assortment of pub and picnic tables. The whimsical outdoor atmosphere carried over to the interior, with brightly painted walls decorated in copper sculptures and stained-glass pieces.

Gavin had wondered why Max would send him to this little bar on an out-of-the-way island, but now he understood the reason for the trip. Max had done this before when he wanted Gavin's opinion on a location. Without giving him any details, he'd send him to "check it out." Gavin would report back with his impression, and, if the two men agreed the place held a unique appeal, they'd mimic its style in one of Holden's resort properties.

This place definitely had a unique appeal.

Had he made the trip alone, he could have a lot of fun roaming around, checking out the artwork, listening to the locals. But he wasn't alone, so he might as well find out what Callie and her friends wanted to drink, hook 'em up, then leave them to get sloshed while he wandered around and soaked up the details.

***

Bartender Sunny Black had her head down in the beer chiller, her arm buried to the elbow in ice, when she heard, "Can I get a blowjob, sex on the beach, and a screaming orgasm, please?"

She rolled her eyes and continued to shift bottles in the cooler without responding. She really needed a better system for taking inventory.

The problem?

Bent over like this, her ass stuck straight up in the air, which seemed to be an open invitation for assholes to hit on her by ordering the raunchiest drink names they could think of. Hard to believe these guys thought she hadn't heard it all before.

She'd been hoping for a quiet night, so she could close up early. But Mr. Hardy-har-har undoubtedly had a posse—jerks always traveled in packs—and they always stayed until last call, using every available minute to get as drunk and obnoxious as possible. She'd be lucky if she got out of here before midnight.

She shifted the Budweisers to the side and resumed counting. *Seven. Eight. Nine. Ten.*

"Ma'am, did you hear me?"

With her free hand, she pulled the Dum-Dum out of her mouth and licked the sticky from her lips. "Look, Romeo," she said, tilting her head so her voice carried to him, rather than echoing around the cooler. "I'll give you five points for a nice, smooth voice. But you lose ten for being a tad overzealous."

She jammed the sucker back into her mouth and resumed counting. *Eleven. Twelve. Thirteen.*

"What the hell are you talking..." His voice trailed off, and then roaring laughter settled over her like thick, heavy honey drizzled on a piping hot biscuit.

He seemed genuinely amused, and she grew curious enough about the man behind the laugh to risk an encouraging look. She leaned back and lifted her head so she could see over the bar.

Holy cow. Even while slurping on a saliva-inducing butterscotch sucker, her mouth went bone dry.

The guy's features were amazing. The Great Sculptor had pressed her thumbs into the flesh of his cheeks, then pulled an upward stroke, leaving behind a slight indention, while at the same time creating high, rugged cheekbones. His square jaw led to a square chin that projected a strong, confident individual. His eyes were like brilliant sapphires, topped by severe dark brows.

His features were sharp, and if not smiling, he would appear harsh, hostile even. But softened by that grin, she found him utterly—and literally—breathtaking.

"I think you misunderstood my request." His eyes twinkled with amusement.

As a bartender, Sunny met good-looking men on a regular basis. Sometimes they tripped her trigger. Most of the time, they didn't. What she felt now catapulted beyond mild interest and ranked more like an internal explosion capable of launching a rocket.

Her flirting game had been packed away so long she wasn't sure she still had it. And if so, she doubted she could find all the pieces. But this guy... he made her want to sort through the game drawer and find as much as possible.

The biting sting of ice—in which her arm was still buried to the elbow—cut through the lustful haze, and her muscle jerked involuntarily. She glanced down, trying to remember what she was doing prior to having her motherboard fried.

Inventory. Right.

Embarrassment over her obvious attraction also had her cheeks burning, and she could only imagine the glow they were putting off. She bit down on the sucker, then tossed the empty stick in the trash can by her feet. "Sorry for being a smart-ass. Let me finish this and"—she smiled, and searched for a flirty tone—"I'll take care of you."

His blue eyes darkened, and his eyelids relaxed. A slow, rakish smile crept across his full lips, causing the tiny cleft in the center of his chin to deepen. "I look forward to that."

Damn. If they weren't talking drinks, this would be the opportunity of a lifetime.

When she finished counting the beers, she patted her arm dry and grabbed three shot glasses off the shelf. She sensed him watching her every move, and her skin heated under his scrutiny. He wasn't excessively tall, maybe six feet, but his presence seemed to dominate her five-foot-four frame.

She wasn't easily intimidated, but the confidence and power he emanated, combined with the raw sexuality she'd glimpsed a moment ago, made her knees weak.

Just once, I want to have sex with a man like that.

God, how she longed for a wild, tumultuous fling that would knock her world off its axis.

Her bracelets jingled and her mouth watered as she shook the canister of whipped cream. What a waste to put it on the drink when she could squirt it on him… then spend an hour or two slowly and deliberately licking it off.

"What's your name?" His voice was huskier than it had been before, and when she met his gaze, the sparks radiating from his blue eyes shot liquid fire straight to her crotch.

"Oh, crap. Was I thinking out loud?"

A smile crawled across his mouth, and her heart stopped. "Nope."

She blew out a breath, then clenched her eyes shut. Even if she hadn't spoken, she was sure she'd broadcast her thoughts like an idiot. This was why she never flirted. She stunk at it. She opened her eyes and cleared her throat. "Sunny. My name's Sunny."

He looked up to the ceiling and said her name a few times, as if trying it on for size. He cocked his head to the side and looked in her eyes. "That's nice."

The charged attraction between them made her jittery as hell. Because of her job, she got hit on often, but she rarely took the bait. At least, nothing more than a little harmless bantering here and there. She had little to no experience in playing sexual games, and it was beyond obvious this man was way out of her league.

She topped the blowjob off with a shot of whipped cream, and then, careful not to let the tremble in her fingers show, set the drinks on a small serving tray. "Sorry you have to carry that yourself. During the winter things are slow, so we don't have wait staff on hand. Well, other than me."

He grinned and reached into his back pocket for his wallet. "I think I can handle the tray." He slid a credit card across the counter, letting go of it only after her fingers brushed his. "Can I run a tab?"

Prickles of awareness and desire wrapped around her fingers and danced up her arm. She knew he'd asked, "Can I run a tab?" but her body heard, "Can I run my hands all over you?"

Lord, she could only imagine what it would be like to have him stroking her skin. The pulsating current ripping through her system would probably cause a meltdown. "Sure. You can…" *Do anything you like.*

Her desire to close up early had evaporated. She'd be more than happy to stick around for as long as he wanted to stay.

She glanced across the bar to where three well-dressed women, two blondes and a brunette, sat. Everyone else in the bar was a local, so they must be the women he'd ordered the drinks for. Sunny made eye contact with the brunette, who, in turn, shot her a what-the-hell-is-taking-so-long glare.

Sunny grinned and cut her eyes to—she glanced at the card in her hand—Gavin McLeod. "You have your hands full with those three."

Okay, had that sounded like she was on a fishing expedition? She hadn't meant it that way, but it would be nice if he volunteered some information regarding his relationship with them. They couldn't all be sisters, could they?

He blew out a harsh breath and pushed his fingers through his thick, black hair. "You have no idea."

A few rebellious locks broke rank and slipped back over his brow, adding a boyish charm to his otherwise severe profile. The impulse to brush the strands off of his forehead was so strong she had to clench her fists at her sides to resist.

Picking up the drink tray, he said, "I'll be right back for my drink. A double shot of Crown." He turned, then stopped and looked back over his shoulder. "Make it a Budweiser, instead." Sunny didn't understand the humor behind his drink request, but based on the glint in his eye and the lopsided grin, the thought of drinking a beer amused him.

As he strode across the hardwood floor toward the waiting women, Sunny stood on tiptoes to get a better view of the full package. An off-white, form-fitting shirt stretched across his broad shoulders and hugged thick biceps, while black, tailor-made slacks hung from a trim waist and encased a nice, tight ass.

Yowzer. She snagged a piece of ice from the cooler and swept it down the side of her neck and across the sharp ridge of her collarbone.

"Damn, girlie. Didn't take much for that fella to get you all hot and bothered."

Sunny scrunched her eyes shut, hunched her shoulders, and hunkered down her head. She'd been so caught up in Gavin, she hadn't thought about Joe and Ed sitting at the end of the bar. Those two old geezers never missed a thing, and they'd be milking this cow forever.

She laughed at the mental image she had of Gavin, stripped, lying on the sacrificial altar of her bar, doused in whipped cream. If she were going to get grief for her actions, wouldn't it be fun to give them something truly amazing to talk about?

About the Author

Alannah believes there's nothing more magical than finding the other half of your soul, experiencing fiery passion, and knowing you've found happily-ever-after.

She loves going to work each day (in sweats and a T-shirt) and writing about hot heroes and feisty heroines who torment each other in the most delicious ways before finding their happy endings.

She lives in the coastal region of North Carolina with her husband, who also happens to be her best friend and biggest fan. They have two sons, a dog, a cat, and an outrageous number of ducks and geese that inhabit the pond on their farm.

www.alannahlynne.com/
www.facebook.com/authoralannahlynne

Other Books by Alannah

Reaction Time

Heat Wave Series

Savin' Me - Book 1
Last Call - Book 2
Crossing Lines - Book 3

Made in the USA
Charleston, SC
12 March 2013